Agatha Christie ®

Death Comes as the End

HarperCollins*Publishers*

HarperCollins*Publishers* Ltd
1 London Bridge Street
London SE1 9GF
www.harpercollins.co.uk

This paperback edition 2017

First published in Great Britain by
Collins, The Crime Club 1944

A catalogue record for this book is available from the British Library

ISBN 978-0-00-819632-5 (PB)
ISBN 978-0-00-825594-7 (POD PB)

Set in Sabon LT Std by Palimpsest Book Production Limited, Falkirk, Stirlingshire

Find out more about HarperCollins and the environment at
www.harpercollins.co.uk/green

TO PROFESSOR S.R.K. GLANVILLE

Dear Stephen,

It was you who originally suggested to me the idea of a detective story set in Ancient Egypt, and but for your active help and encouragement this book would never have been written.

I want to say here how much I have enjoyed all the interesting literature you have lent me and to thank you once more for the patience with which you have answered my questions and for the time and trouble you have expended. The pleasure and interest which the writing of the book has brought to me you already know.

Your affectionate and grateful friend,

Agatha Christie

Contents

Author's Note

The action of this book takes place on the West bank of the Nile at Thebes in Egypt about 2000 BC. Both place and time are incidental to the story. Any other place at any other time would have served as well: but it so happened that the inspiration of both characters and plot was derived from two or three Egyptian letters of the XI Dynasty, found about 20 years ago by the Egyptian Expedition of the Metropolitan Museum of Art, New York, in a rock tomb opposite Luxor, and translated by Professor (then Mr) Battiscombe Gunn in the Museum's Bulletin.

It may be of interest to the reader to note that an endowment for *Ka*service—an everyday feature of ancient Egyptian civilization—was very similar in principle to a mediæval chantry bequest. Property was bequeathed to the *Ka*-priest in return for which he was expected to maintain the tomb of the testator, and to provide offerings at the tomb on certain feast days throughout the year for the repose of the deceased's soul.

The terms 'Brother', 'Sister' in Egyptian texts, regularly

1

mean 'Lover' and are frequently interchangeable with 'Husband', 'Wife'. They are so used on occasion in this book.

The Agricultural calendar of Ancient Egypt, consisting of three seasons of four months of thirty days, formed the background of peasant life, and with the addition of five intercalary days at the end of the year was used as the official calendar of 365 days to the year. This 'Year' originally began with the arrival in Egypt of the flood-water of the Nile in the third week of July by our reckoning; but the absence of a Leap Year caused it to lag through the centuries, so that, at the time of our story, the official New Year's Day fell about six months earlier than the opening of the agricultural year, i.e. in January instead of July. To save the reader from continually having to make allowance for this six months, however, the dates here used as Chapter headings are stated in terms of the agricultural year of the time, i.e. Inundation—late July to late November; Winter—late November to late March; and Summer—late March to late July.

A.C. 1944

PART ONE

Inundation

CHAPTER 1

Second Month of Inundation 20th Day

Renisenb stood looking over the Nile.

In the distance she could hear faintly the upraised voices of her brothers, Yahmose and Sobek, disputing as to whether or no the dykes in a certain place needed strengthening or not. Sobek's voice was high and confident as always. He had the habit of asserting his views with easy certainty. Yahmose's voice was low and grumbling in tone, it expressed doubt and anxiety. Yahmose was always in a state of anxiety over something or other. He was the eldest son, and during his father's absence on the Northern Estates the management of the farmlands was more or less in his hands. Yahmose was slow, prudent and prone to look for difficulties where none existed. He was a heavily built, slow moving man with none of Sobek's gaiety and confidence.

From her early childhood Renisenb could remember hearing these elder brothers of hers arguing in just those selfsame accents. It gave her suddenly a feeling of security . . . She was at home again. Yes, she had come home . . .

Yet as she looked once more across the pale, shining river, her rebellion and pain mounted again. Khay, her young husband, was dead . . . Khay with his laughing face and his strong shoulders. Khay was with Osiris in the Kingdom of the dead—and she, Renisenb, his dearly loved wife, was left desolate. Eight years they had had together—she had come to him as little more than a child—and now she had returned widowed, with Khay's child, Teti, to her father's house.

It seemed to her at this moment as though she had never been away . . .

She welcomed that thought . . .

She would forget those eight years—so full of unthinking happiness, so torn and destroyed by loss and pain.

Yes, forget them, put them out of her mind. Become once more Renisenb, Imhotep the ka-priest's daughter, the unthinking, unfeeling girl. This love of a husband and brother had been a cruel thing, deceiving her by its sweetness. She remembered the strong bronze shoulders, the laughing mouth—now Khay was embalmed, swathed in bandages, protected with amulets in his journey through the other world. No more Khay in this world to sail on the Nile and catch fish and laugh up into the sun whilst she, stretched out in the boat with little Teti on her lap, laughed back at him . . .

Renisenb thought:

'I will not think of it. It is over! Here I am at home. Everything is the same as it was. I, too, shall be the same presently. It will all be as before. Teti has forgotten already. She plays with the other children and laughs.'

Renisenb turned abruptly and made her way back towards the house, passing on the way some loaded donkeys being driven towards the river bank. She passed by the cornbins and the outhouses and through the gateway into the courtyard. It was very pleasant in the courtyard. There was the artificial lake, surrounded by flowering oleanders and jasmines and shaded by sycamore fig trees. Teti and the other children were playing there now, their voices rising shrill and clear. They were running in and out of the little pavilion that stood at one side of the lake. Renisenb noticed that Teti was playing with a wooden lion whose mouth opened and shut by pulling a string, a toy which she herself had loved as a child. She thought again, gratefully, 'I have come home . . .' Nothing was changed here, all was as it had been. Here life was safe, constant, unchanging. Teti was now the child and she one of the many mothers enclosed by the home walls—but the framework, the essence of things, was unchanged.

A ball with which one of the children was playing rolled to her feet and she picked it up and threw it back, laughing.

Renisenb went on to the porch with its gaily coloured columns, and then through into the house, passing through the big central chamber, with its coloured frieze of lotus and poppies and so on to the back of the house and the women's quarters.

Upraised voices struck on her ear and she paused again, savouring with pleasure the old familiar echoes. Satipy and Kait—arguing as always! Those well-remembered tones of Satipy's voice, high, domineering and bullying! Satipy was her brother Yahmose's wife, a tall, energetic, loud-tongued woman, handsome in a hard, commanding kind of way. She was eternally laying down the law, hectoring the servants, finding fault with everything, getting impossible things done by sheer force of vituperation and personality. Everyone dreaded her tongue and ran to obey her orders. Yahmose himself had the greatest admiration for his resolute, spirited wife, though he allowed himself to be bullied by her in a way that had often infuriated Renisenb.

At intervals, in the pauses in Satipy's high-pitched sentences, the quiet, obstinate voice of Kait was heard. Kait was a broad, plain-faced woman, the wife of the handsome, gay Sobek. She was devoted to her children and seldom thought or spoke about anything else. She sustained her side of the daily arguments with her sister-in-law by the simple expedient of repeating whatever statement she had originally made with quiet, immovable obstinacy. She displayed neither heat nor passion, and never considered for a moment any side of a question but her own. Sobek was extremely attached to his wife and talked freely to her of all his affairs, secure in the knowledge that she would appear to listen, make comforting sounds of assent or dissent, and would remember nothing inconvenient, since her mind was sure to have been dwelling on some problem connected with the children all the time.

'It's an outrage, that's what I say,' shouted Satipy. 'If Yahmose had the spirit of a mouse he would not stand it for a moment! Who is in charge here when Imhotep is absent? Yahmose! And as Yahmose's wife it is *I* who should have the first choice of the woven mats and cushions. That hippopotamus of a black slave should be—'

Kait's heavy, deep voice cut in:

'No, no, my little one, do not eat your doll's hair. See, here is something better—a sweet—oh, how *good* . . .'

'As for you, Kait, you have no courtesy, you don't even listen to what I say—you do not reply—your manners are atrocious.'

'The blue cushion has always been mine . . . Oh look at little Ankh—she is trying to walk . . .'

'You are as stupid as your children, Kait, and that is saying a good deal! But you shall not get out of it like this. I will have my rights, I tell you.'

Renisenb started as a quiet footfall sounded behind her. She turned with a start and with the old, familiar feeling of dislike at seeing the woman Henet standing behind her.

Henet's thin face was twisted into its usual half-cringing smile.

'Things haven't changed much, you'll be thinking, Renisenb,' she said. 'How we all bear Satipy's tongue, I don't know! Of course, Kait can answer back. Some of us aren't so fortunate! I know *my* place, I hope—and my gratitude to your father for giving me a home and food and clothing. Ah, he's a good man, your father. And I've always tried to do what I can. I'm always working—giving a hand here and a hand there—and I don't expect thanks or gratitude. If your dear mother had lived it would have been different. *She* appreciated me. Like sisters we were! A beautiful woman she was. Well, I've done my duty and kept my promise to her. "Look after the children, Henet," she said when she was dying. And I've been faithful to my word. Slaved for you all, I have, and never wanted thanks. Neither asked for them nor got them! "It's only old Henet," people say, "she doesn't count." Nobody thinks anything of me. Why should they? I just try and be helpful, that's all.'

She slipped like an eel under Renisenb's arm and entered the inner room.

'About these cushions, you'll excuse me, Satipy, but I happened to hear Sobek say—'

Renisenb moved away. Her old dislike of Henet surged up. Funny how they all disliked Henet! It was her whining voice, her continual self-pity and the occasional malicious pleasure she took in fanning the flames of a discussion.

'Oh well,' thought Renisenb, 'why not?' It was, she supposed, Henet's way of amusing herself. Life must be dreary for her—and it was true that she worked like a drudge and that no one was ever grateful. You couldn't be grateful to Henet—she drew attention to her own merits so persistently that it chilled any generous response you might have felt.

Henet, thought Renisenb, was one of those people whose fate it is to be devoted to others and to have no one devoted to them. She was unattractive to look at, and stupid as well. Yet she always knew what was going on. Her noise-less way of walking, her sharp ears, and her quick peering eyes made it a certainty that nothing could long be a secret from her. Sometimes she hugged her knowledge to herself— at other times she would go around from one person to another, whispering, and standing back delightedly to observe the results of her tale-telling.

At one time or another everyone in the household had

begged Imhotep to get rid of Henet, but Imhotep would never hear of such a thing. He was perhaps the only person who was fond of her; and she repaid his patronage with a fulsome devotion that the rest of the family found quite nauseating.

Renisenb stood uncertainly for a moment, listening to the accelerated clamour of her sisters-in-law, fanned by the flame of Henet's interference, then she went slowly towards the small room where her grandmother, Esa, sat by herself, attended by two little black slave girls. She was busy now inspecting certain linen garments that they were displaying to her and scolding them in a characteristic, friendly fashion.

Yes, it was all the same. Renisenb stood, unnoticed, listening. Old Esa had shrunk a little, that was all. But her voice was the same and the things that she was saying were the same, word for word, almost, as Renisenb could remember them before she herself had left home eight years ago . . .

Renisenb slipped out again. Neither the old woman nor the two little black slave girls had noticed her. For a moment or two Renisenb paused by the open kitchen door. A smell of roasting ducks, a lot of talking and laughing and scolding all going on at once; a mound of vegetables waiting to be prepared.

Renisenb stood quite still, her eyes half closed. From where she stood she could hear everything going on at once. The rich, varied noises of the kitchen, the high, shrill note of old Esa's voice, the strident tones of Satipy and, very faintly, the deeper, persistent contralto of Kait. A babel of women's voices—chattering, laughing, complaining, scolding, exclaiming . . .

And suddenly Renisenb felt stifled, encircled by this persistent and clamorous femininity. Women—noisy, vociferous women! A houseful of women—never quiet, never peaceful—always talking, exclaiming, *saying* things—not *doing* them!

And Khay—Khay silent and watchful in his boat, his whole mind bent on the fish he was going to spear . . .

None of this clack of tongues, this busy, incessant *fussiness*.

Renisenb went swiftly out of the house again into hot, clear stillness. She saw Sobek coming back from the fields and saw in the distance Yahmose going up towards the Tomb.

She turned away and took the path up to the limestone cliffs where the Tomb was. It was the Tomb of the great Noble Meriptah and her father was the mortuary priest responsible for its upkeep. All the estate and land was part of the endowment of the Tomb.

When her father was away the duties of the ka-priest fell upon her brother Yahmose. When Renisenb, walking slowly up the steep path, arrived, Yahmose was in consultation with Hori, her father's man of business and affairs, in a little rock chamber next door to the offering chamber of the Tomb.

Hori had a sheet of papyrus spread out on his knees and Yahmose and he were bending over it.

Both Yahmose and Hori smiled at Renisenb when she arrived and she sat down near them in a patch of shade.

She had always been very fond of her brother Yahmose. He was gentle and affectionate to her and had a mild and kindly disposition. Hori, too, had always been gravely kind to the small Renisenb and had sometimes mended her toys for her. He had been a grave, silent young man when she went away, with sensitive, clever fingers. Renisenb thought that though he looked older he had changed hardly at all. The grave smile he gave her was just the same as she remembered.

Yahmose and Hori were murmuring together:

'Seventy-three bushels of barley with Ipi the younger . . .'

'The total then is two hundred and thirty of spelt and one hundred and twenty of barley.'

'Yes, but there is the price of the timber, and the crop was paid for in oil at Perhaa . . .'

Their talk went on. Renisenb sat drowsily content with the men's murmuring voices as a background. Presently Yahmose got up and went away, handing back the roll of papyrus to Hori.

Renisenb sat on in a companionable silence.

Presently she touched a roll of papyrus and asked: 'Is that from my father?'

Hori nodded.

'What does he say?' she asked curiously.

She unrolled it and stared at those marks that were meaningless to her untutored eyes.

Smiling a little, Hori leaned over her shoulder and traced with his finger as he read. The letter was couched in the ornate style of the professional letter writer of Heracleopolis.

13

Agatha Christie

'The Servant of the Estate, the Ka servant Imhotep says:
    'May your condition be like that of one who lives a
million times. May the God Herishaf, Lord of
Heracleopolis and all the Gods that are aid you. May the
God Ptah gladden your heart as one who lives long. The
son speaks to his mother, the Ka servant to his mother
Esa. How are you in your life, safety and health? To the
whole household, how are you? To my son Yahmose,
how are you in your life, safety and health? Make the
most of my land. Strive to the uttermost, dig the ground
with your noses in the work. See, if you are industrious
I will praise God for you—'

Renisenb laughed.

'Poor Yahmose! He works hard enough, I am sure.'

Her father's exhortations had brought him vividly before
her eyes—his pompous, slightly fussy manner, his continual
exhortations and instructions.

Hori went on:

*Take great care of my son Ipy. I hear he is discontented.
Also see that Satipy treats Henet well. Mind this. Do not
fail to write about the flax and the oil. Guard the
produce of my grain—guard everything of mine, for I
shall hold you responsible. If my land floods, woe to you
and Sobek.'*

'My father is just the same,' said Renisenb happily. 'Always
thinking that nothing can be done right if he is not here.'

She let the roll of papyrus slip and added softly:

14

'Everything is just the same . . .'

Hori did not answer.

He took up a sheet of papyrus and began to write. Renisenb watched him lazily for some time. She felt too contented to speak.

By and by she said dreamily:

'It would be interesting to know how to write on papyrus. Why doesn't everyone learn?'

'It is not necessary.'

'Not necessary, perhaps, but it would be pleasant.'

'You think so, Renisenb? What difference would it make to *you*?'

Renisenb slowly considered for a moment or two. Then she said slowly:

'When you ask me like that, truly I do not know, Hori.'

Hori said, 'At present a few scribes are all that are needed on a large estate, but the day will come, I fancy, when there will be armies of scribes all over Egypt.'

'That will be a good thing,' said Renisenb.

Hori said slowly: 'I am not so sure.'

'Why are you not sure?'

'Because, Renisenb, it is so easy and it costs so little labour to write down ten bushels of barley, or a hundred head of cattle, or ten fields of spelt—and the thing that is written will come to seem like the real thing, and so the writer and the scribe will come to despise the man who ploughs the fields and reaps the barley and raises the cattle—but all the same the fields and the cattle are *real*— they are not just marks of ink on papyrus. And when all the records and all the papyrus rolls are destroyed and the scribes are scattered, the men who toil and reap will go on, and Egypt will still live.'

Renisenb looked at him attentively. She said slowly: 'Yes, I see what you mean. Only the things that you can *see* and *touch* and *eat* are real . . . To write down "I have two hundred and forty bushels of barley" means nothing unless you *have* the barley. One could write down lies.'

Hori smiled at her serious face. Renisenb said suddenly: 'You mended my lion for me—long ago, do you remember?'

'Yes, I remember, Renisenb.'

'Teti is playing with it now . . . It is the same lion.'

She paused and then said simply:

'When Khay went to Osiris I was very sad. But now I have come home and I shall be happy again and forget— for everything here is the same. Nothing is changed at all.'

'You really think that?'

Renisenb looked at him sharply.

'What do you mean, Hori?'

'I mean there is always change. Eight years is eight years.'

'Nothing changes here,' said Renisenb with confidence.

'Perhaps then, there *should* be change.'

Renisenb said sharply:

'No, no, I want everything the same!'

'But you yourself are not the same Renisenb who went away with Khay.'

'Yes I am! Or if not, then I soon shall be again.'

Hori shook his head.

'You cannot go back, Renisenb. It is like my measures here. I take half and add to it a quarter, and then a tenth and then a twenty-fourth—and at the end, you see, it is a different quantity altogether.'

'But I am just Renisenb.'

'But Renisenb has something added to her all the time, so she becomes all the time a different Renisenb!'

'No, no. You are the same Hori.'

'You may think so, but it is not so.'

'Yes, yes, and Yahmose is the same, so worried and so anxious, and Satipy bullies him just the same, and she and Kait were having their usual quarrel about mats or beads, and presently when I go back they will be laughing together, the best of friends, and Henet still creeps about and listens and whines about her devotion, and my grandmother was fussing with her little maid over some linen! It was all the same, and presently my father will come home and there will be a great fuss, and he will say "why have you not done this?" and "you should have done that," and Yahmose will look worried and Sobek will laugh and be insolent about it, and my father will spoil Ipy who is sixteen just as he used to spoil him when he was eight, and nothing will be different at all!' She paused, breathless.

Hori sighed. Then he said gently:

'You do not understand, Renisenb. There is an evil that comes from outside, that attacks so that all the world can see, but there is another kind of rottenness that breeds from within—that shows no outward sign. It grows slowly, day by day, till at last the whole fruit is rotten—eaten away by disease.'

Renisenb stared at him. He had spoken almost absently, not as though he were speaking to her, but more like a man who muses to himself.

She cried out sharply:

'What do you mean, Hori? You make me afraid.'

'I am afraid myself.'

'But what do you *mean*? What is this evil you talk about?'

He looked at her then, and suddenly smiled.

'Forget what I said, Renisenb. I was thinking of the diseases that attack the crops.'

Renisenb sighed in relief.

'I'm glad. I thought—I don't know what I thought.'

CHAPTER 2

Third Month of Inundation 4th Day

Satipy was talking to Yahmose. Her voice had a high strident note that seldom varied its tone.

'You must assert yourself. That is what I say! You will never be valued unless you assert yourself. Your father says this must be done and that must be done and why have you not done the others? And you listen meekly and reply yes, yes, and excuse yourself for the things that he says should have been done—and which, the Gods know, have often been quite impossible! Your father treats you as a child—as a young, irresponsible boy! You might be the age of Ipy.'

Yahmose said quietly:

'My father does not treat me in the least as he treats Ipy.'

'No, indeed.' Satipy fell upon the new subject with renewed venom. 'He is foolish about that spoiled brat! Day by day Ipy gets more impossible. He swaggers round and does no work that he can help and pretends that anything that is asked of him is too hard for him! It is a disgrace.

And all because he knows that your father will always indulge him and take his part. You and Sobek should take a strong line about it.'

Yahmose shrugged his shoulders.

'What is the good?'

'You drive me mad, Yahmose—that is so like you! You have no *spirit*. You're as meek as a woman! Everything that your father says you agree with at once!'

'I have a great affection for my father.'

'Yes, and he trades on that! You go on meekly accepting blame and excusing yourself for things that are no fault of yours! You should speak up and answer him back as Sobek does. Sobek is afraid of nobody!'

'Yes, but remember, Satipy, that it is *I* who am trusted by my father, not Sobek. My father reposes no confidence in Sobek. Everything is always left to *my* judgement, not his.'

'And that is why you should be definitely associated as a partner in the estate! You represent your father when he is away, you act as ka-priest in his absence, everything is left in your hands—and yet you have no recognized authority. There should be a proper settlement. You are now a man of nearly middle age. It's not right that you should be treated still as a child.'

Yahmose said doubtfully:

'My father likes to keep things in his own hands.'

'Exactly. It pleases him that everyone in the household should be dependent upon him—and upon his whim of the moment. It is bad, that, and it will get worse. This time when he comes home you must tackle him boldly—you must say that you demand a settlement in writing, that you insist on having a regularized position.'

'He would not listen.'

'Then you must *make* him listen. Oh that I were a man! If I were in your place *I* would know what to do! Sometimes I feel that I am married to a worm.'

Yahmose flushed.

'I will see what I can do—I might, yes, I might perhaps speak to my father—ask him—'

'Not *ask*—you must *demand*! After all, you have the whip hand of him. There is no one but you whom he can leave in charge here. Sobek is too wild, your father does not trust him, and Ipy is too young.'

'There is always Hori.'

'Hori is not a member of the family. Your father relies on his judgement, but he would not leave authority except in the hands of his own kin. But I see how it is; you are too meek and mild—and there is milk in your veins, not blood! You don't consider me, or our children. Not till your father is dead shall we ever have our proper position.'

Yahmose said heavily:

'You despise me, don't you, Satipy?'

'You make me angry.'

'Listen, I tell you that I will speak to my father when he comes. There, it is a promise.'

Satipy murmured under her breath:

'Yes—but *how* will you speak? Like a man—or like a mouse?'

*

21

Kait was playing with her youngest child, little Ankh. The baby was just beginning to walk and Kait encouraged her with laughing words, kneeling in front of her and waiting with outstretched arms until the child lurched precariously forward and toddled on uncertain feet into her mother's arms.

Kait had been displaying these accomplishments to Sobek, but she realized suddenly that he was not attending, but was sitting with his handsome forehead furrowed into a frown.

'Oh, Sobek—you were not looking. You do not see. Little one, tell your father he is naughty not to watch you.'

Sobek said irritably:

'I have other things to think of—yes, and worry about.'

Kait leaned back on her heels, smoothing her hair back from her heavy dark brows where Ankh's fingers had clutched it.

'Why? Is there something wrong?'

Kait spoke without quite giving all her attention. The question was more than half mechanical.

Sobek said angrily:

'The trouble is that I am not trusted. My father is an old man, absurdly old-fashioned in his ideas, and he insists on dictating every single action here—he will not leave things to my judgement.'

Kait shook her head and murmured vaguely:

'Yes, yes, it is too bad.'

'If only Yahmose had a little more spirit and would back me up there might be some hope of making my father see reason. But Yahmose is so timid. He carries out every single instruction my father gives him to the letter.'

Kait jingled some beads at the child and murmured:

'Yes, that is true.'

'In this matter of the timber I shall tell my father when he comes that I used my judgement. It was far better to take the price in flax and not in oil.'

'I am sure you are right.'

'But my father is as obstinate over having his own way as anyone can be. He will make an outcry, will shout out, "I told you to transact the business in oil. Everything is done wrong when I am not here. You are a foolish boy who knows nothing!" How old does he think I am? He doesn't realize that I am now a man in my prime and he is past his. His instructions and his refusals to sanction any unusual transactions mean that we do not do nearly as good business as we might do. To attain riches it is necessary to take a few risks. I have vision and courage. My father has neither.'

Her eyes on the child, Kait murmured softly:

'You are so bold and so clever, Sobek.'

'But he shall hear some home truths this time if he dares to find fault and shout abuse at me! Unless I am given a free hand I shall leave. I shall go away.'

Kait, her hand stretched out to the child, turned her head sharply, the gesture arrested.

'Go away? Where would you go?'

'Somewhere! It is insupportable to be bullied and nagged at by a fussy, self-important old man who gives me no scope at all to show what I can do.'

'No,' said Kait sharply. 'I say no, Sobek.'

He stared at her, recalled by her tone into noticing her

23

Agatha Christie

presence. He was so used to her as a merely soothing accompaniment to his talk that he often forgot her existence as a living, thinking, human woman.

'What do you mean, Kait?'

'I mean that I will not let you be foolish. All the estate belongs to your father, the lands, the cultivation, the cattle, the timber, the fields of flax—all! When your father dies it will be ours—yours and Yahmose's and our children's. If you quarrel with your father and go off, then he may divide your share between Yahmose and Ipy—already he loves Ipy too much. Ipy knows that and trades on it. You must not play into the hands of Ipy. It would suit him only too well if you were to quarrel with Imhotep and go away. We have our children to think of.'

Sobek stared at her. Then he gave a short surprised laugh.

'A woman is always unexpected. I did not know you had it in you, Kait, to be so fierce.'

Kait said earnestly:

'Do not quarrel with your father. Do not answer him back. Be wise for a little longer.'

'Perhaps you are right—but this may go on for years. What my father should do is to associate us with him in a partnership.'

Kait shook her head.

'He will not do that. He likes too much to say that we are all eating his bread, that we are all dependent on him, that without him we should all be nowhere.'

Sobek looked at her curiously.

'You do not like my father very much, Kait.'

But Kait had bent once more to the toddling baby.

'Come, sweetheart—see, here is your doll. Come, then—come . . .'

Sobek looked down at her black bent head. Then, with a puzzled look, he went out.

Esa had sent for her grandson Ipy.

The boy, a handsome, discontented-looking stripling, was standing before her whilst she rated him in a high shrill voice, peering at him out of her dim eyes that were shrewd although they could now see little.

'What is this I hear? You will not do this, and you will not do that? You want to look after the bulls, and you do not like going with Yahmose or seeing to the cultivating? What are things coming to when a child like you says what he will or will not do?'

Ipy said sullenly:

'I am not a child. I am grown now—and why should I be treated as a child? Put to this work or that with no say of my own and no separate allowance. Given orders all the time by Yahmose. Who does Yahmose think he is?'

'He is your older brother and he is in charge here when my son Imhotep is away.'

'Yahmose is stupid, slow and stupid. I am much cleverer than he is. And Sobek is stupid too for all that he boasts and talks about how clever he is! Already my father has written and has said that I am to do the work that I myself choose—'

'Which is none at all,' interpolated old Esa.

'And that I am to be given more food and drink, and

25

that if he hears I am discontented and have not been well treated he will be very angry.'

He smiled as he spoke, a sly upcurving smile.

'You are a spoiled brat,' said Esa with energy. 'And I shall tell Imhotep so.'

'No, no, grandmother, you would not do that.'

His smile changed, it became caressing if slightly impudent.

'You and I, grandmother, we have the brains of the family.'

'The impudence of you!'

'My father relies on your judgement—he knows you are wise.'

'That may be—indeed it is so—but I do not need you to tell me so.'

Ipy laughed.

'You had better be on my side, grandmother.'

'What is this talk of *sides*?'

'The big brothers are very discontented, don't you know that? Of course you do. Henet tells you everything. Satipy harangues Yahmose all day and all night whenever she can get hold of him. And Sobek has made a fool of himself over the sale of the timber and is afraid my father will be furious when he finds out. You see, grandmother, in another year or two *I* shall be associated with my father and he will do everything that I wish.'

'You, the youngest of the family?'

'What does age matter? My father is the one that has the power—and I am the one who knows how to manage my father!'

'This is evil talk,' said Esa.

Ipy said softly: 'You are not a fool, grandmother . . . You know quite well that my father, in spite of all his big talk, is really a weak man—'

He stopped abruptly, noting that Esa had shifted her head and was peering over his shoulder. He turned his own head, to find Henet standing close behind him.

'So Imhotep is a weak man?' said Henet in her soft whining voice. 'He will not be pleased, I think, to hear that you have said *that* of him.'

Ipy gave a quick uneasy laugh.

'But you will not tell him, Henet . . . Come now, Henet—promise me . . . Dear Henet . . .'

Henet glided towards Esa. She raised her voice with its slightly whining note.

'Of course, I never want to make trouble—you know that . . . I am devoted to all of you. I never repeat anything unless I think it is my *duty* . . .'

'I was teasing grandmother, that was all,' said Ipy. 'I shall tell my father so. He will know I could not have said such a thing seriously.'

He gave Henet a short, sharp nod and went out of the room.

Henet looked after him and said to Esa:

'A fine boy—a fine, well-grown boy. And how bravely he speaks!'

Esa said sharply:

'He speaks dangerously. I do not like the ideas he has in his head. My son indulges him too much.'

'Who would not? He is such a handsome, attractive boy.'

'Handsome is as handsome does,' said Esa sharply.

She was silent a moment or two, then she said slowly: 'Henet—I am worried.'

'Worried, Esa? What would worry you? Anyway, the master will soon be here and then all will be well.'

'Will it? I wonder.'

She was silent once more, then she said:

'Is my grandson Yahmose in the house?'

'I saw him coming towards the porch a few moments ago.'

'Go and tell him I wish to speak with him.'

Henet departed. She found Yahmose on the cool porch with its gaily coloured columns and gave him Esa's message.

Yahmose obeyed the summons at once.

Esa said abruptly:

'Yahmose, very soon Imhotep will be here.'

Yahmose's gentle face lighted up.

'Yes, that will indeed be good.'

'All is in order for him? Affairs have prospered?'

'My father's instructions have been carried out as well as I could compass them.'

'What of Ipy?'

Yahmose sighed.

'My father is over-indulgent where that boy is concerned. It is not good for the lad.'

'You must make that clear to Imhotep.'

Yahmose looked doubtful.

Esa said firmly: 'I will back you up.'

'Sometimes,' said Yahmose, sighing, 'there seems to be nothing but difficulties. But everything will be right when my father comes. He can make his own decisions then. It is hard to act as he would wish in his absence—especially when I have no authority, and only act as his delegate.'

Esa said slowly:

'You are a good son—loyal and affectionate. You have been a good husband too, you have obeyed the proverb that says that a man should love his wife and make a home for her, that he should fill her belly and put clothes on her back, and provide expensive ointments for her toilet and that he should gladden her heart as long as she lives. But there is a further precept—it goes like this: *Prevent her from getting the mastery*. If I were you, grandson, I should take that precept to heart . . .'

Yahmose looked at her, flushed deeply and turned away.

CHAPTER 3

Third Month of Inundation 14th Day

Everywhere there was bustle and preparation. Hundreds of loaves had been baked in the kitchen, now ducks were roasting; there was a smell of leeks and garlic and various spices. Women were shouting and giving orders, serving men ran to and fro.

Everywhere ran the murmur:

'The master—the master is coming . . .'

Renisenb, helping to weave garlands of poppies and lotus flowers, felt an excited happiness bubbling up in her heart. Her father was coming home! In the last few weeks she had slipped imperceptibly back into the confines of her old life. That first sense of unfamiliarity and strangeness, induced in her, she believed, by Hori's words, had gone. She was the same Renisenb—Yahmose, Satipy, Sobek and Kait were all the same—now, as in the past, there was all the bustle and fuss of preparations for Imhotep's return. Word had come ahead that he would be with them before nightfall. One of the servants had been posted on the river bank to give warning of the master's approach, and suddenly his voice rang out loud and clear giving the agreed call.

Renisenb dropped her flowers and ran out with the others. They all hastened towards the mooring place on the river bank. Yahmose and Sobek were already there in a little crowd of villagers, fishermen and farm labourers, all calling out excitedly and pointing.

Yes, there was the barge with its great square sail coming fast up the river with the North wind bellying out the sail. Close behind it was the kitchen barge crowded with men and women. Presently Renisenb could make out her father sitting holding a lotus flower and with him someone whom she took to be a singer.

The cries on the bank redoubled, Imhotep waved a welcoming hand, the sailors were heaving and pulling on the halyards. There were cries of 'Welcome to the master,' calls upon the Gods, and thanks for his safe return, and a few moments later Imhotep came ashore, greeting his family and answering the loud salutations that etiquette demanded.

'Praise be to Sobek, the child of Neith, who has brought you safely on the water!' 'Praise be to Ptah, south of the Memphite wall, who brings you to us! Thanks be to Ré who illumines the Two Lands!'

Renisenb pressed forward, intoxicated with the general excitement.

Imhotep drew himself up importantly and suddenly Renisenb thought: 'But he is a *small* man. I thought of him as much bigger than that.'

A feeling that was almost dismay passed over her.

Had her father *shrunk*? Or was her own memory at

fault? She thought of him as rather a splendid being, tyrannical, often fussy, exhorting everybody right and left, and sometimes provoking her to quiet inward laughter, but nevertheless a *personage*. But this small, stout, elderly man, looking so full of his own importance and yet somehow failing to impress—what was wrong with her? What were these disloyal thoughts that came into her head?

Imhotep, having finished the sonorous and ceremonial phrases, had arrived at the stage of more personal greetings. He embraced his sons.

'Ah, my good Yahmose, all smiles, you have been diligent in my absence, I am sure . . . And Sobek, my handsome son, still given to merriness of heart, I see. And here is Ipy—my dearest Ipy—let me look at you—stand away—so. Grown bigger, more of a man, how it rejoices my heart to hold you again! And Renisenb—my dear daughter—once more in the home. Satipy, Kait, my no less dear daughters . . . And Henet—my faithful Henet—'

Henet was kneeling, embracing his knees, and ostentatiously wiping tears of joy from her eyes.

'It is good to see you, Henet—you are well—happy? As devoted as ever—that is pleasant to the heart . . .

'And my excellent Hori, so clever with his accounts and his pen! All has prospered? I am sure it has.'

Then, the greetings finished and the surrounding murmur dying down, Imhotep raised his hand for silence and spoke out loud and clear.

'My sons and daughters—friends. I have a piece of news for you. For many years, as you all know, I have been a lonely man in one respect. My wife (your mother, Yahmose and Sobek) and my sister (your mother, Ipy) have both gone to Osiris many years ago. So to you, Satipy and Kait, I bring a new sister to share your home. Behold, this is my concubine, Nofret, whom you shall love for my sake. She has come with me from Memphis in the North and will dwell here with you when I go away again.'

As he spoke he drew forward a woman by the hand. She stood there beside him, her head flung back, her eyes narrowed, young, arrogant and beautiful.

Renisenb thought, with a shock of surprise: 'But she's quite young—perhaps not as old as I am.'

Nofret stood quite still. There was a faint smile on her lips—it had more derision in it than any anxiety to please.

She had very straight black brows and a rich bronze skin, and her eyelashes were so long and thick that one could hardly see her eyes.

The family, taken aback, stared in dumb silence. With a faint edge of irritation in his voice, Imhotep said:

'Come now, children, welcome Nofret. Don't you know how to greet your father's concubine when he brings her to his house?'

Haltingly and stumblingly the greetings were given.

Imhotep, affecting a heartiness that perhaps concealed some uneasiness, exclaimed cheerfully:

'That's better! Nofret, Satipy and Kait and Renisenb will take you to the women's quarters. Where are the trunks? Have the trunks been brought ashore?'

The round-topped travelling trunks were being carried from the barge. Imhotep said to Nofret:

Agatha Christie

'Your jewels and your clothes are here safely. Go and see to their bestowing.'

Then, as the women moved away together, he turned to his sons.

'And what of the estate? Does all go well?'

'The lower fields that were rented to Nakht—' began Yahmose, but his father cut him short.

'No details now, good Yahmose. They can wait. Tonight is rejoicing. Tomorrow you and I and Hori here will get to business. Come, Ipy, my boy, let us walk to the house. How tall you have grown—your head is above mine.'

Scowling, Sobek walked behind his father and Ipy. Into Yahmose's ear he murmured:

'Jewels and clothes—did you hear? That is where the profits of the Northern estates have gone. *Our* profits.'

'Hush,' whispered Yahmose. 'Our father will hear.'

'What if he does? I am not afraid of him as you are.'

Once in the house, Henet came to Imhotep's room to prepare the bath. She was all smiles.

Imhotep abandoned a little of his defensive heartiness.

'Well, Henet, and what do you think of my choice?'

Although he had determined to carry things off with a high hand, he had known quite well that the arrival of Nofret would provoke a storm—at least in the women's part of the house. Henet was different. A singularly devoted creature. She did not disappoint him.

'She is beautiful! Quite beautiful! What hair, what limbs! She is worthy of you, Imhotep, what can I say more than that? Your dear wife who is dead will be glad that you have chosen such a companion to gladden your days.'

34

'You think so, Henet?'

'I am sure of it, Imhotep. After mourning her so many years it is time that you once more enjoyed life.'

'You knew her well . . . I, too, felt it was time to live as a man should live. Er ahem—my sons' wives and my daughter—they will take this with resentment perhaps?'

'They had better not,' said Henet. 'After all, do they not all depend upon you in this house?'

'Very true, very true,' said Imhotep.

'Your bounty feeds and clothes them—their welfare is entirely the result of your efforts.'

'Yes, indeed.' Imhotep sighed. 'I am continually active on their behalf. I sometimes doubt if they realize all they owe to me.'

'You must remind them of it,' said Henet, nodding her head. 'I, your humble devoted Henet, never forget what I owe you—but children are sometimes thoughtless and selfish, thinking, perhaps, that it is *they* who are important and not realizing that they only carry out the instructions that *you* give.'

'That is indeed most true,' said Imhotep. 'I have always said you were an intelligent creature, Henet.'

Henet sighed. 'If others only thought so.'

'What is this? Has anyone been unkind to you?'

'No, no—that is, they do not mean it—it is a matter of course to them that I should work unceasingly (which I am glad to do)—but a word of affection and appreciation, that is what makes all the difference.'

'That you will always have from me,' said Imhotep. 'And this is always your home, remember.'

'You are too kind, master.' She paused and added: 'The slaves are ready in the bathroom with the hot water—and when you have bathed and dressed, your mother asks that you should go to her.'

'Ah, my mother? Yes—yes, of course . . .'

Imhotep looked suddenly slightly embarrassed. He covered his confusion by saying quickly:

'Naturally—I had intended that—tell Esa I shall come.'

Esa, dressed in her best pleated linen gown, peered across at her son with a kind of sardonic amusement.

'Welcome, Imhotep. So you have returned to us—and not alone, I hear.'

Imhotep, drawing himself up, replied rather shamefacedly:

'Oh, so you have heard?'

'Naturally. The house is humming with the news. The girl is beautiful, they say, and quite young.'

'She is nineteen and—er—not ill looking.'

Esa laughed—an old woman's spiteful cackle.

'Ah, well,' she said, 'there's no fool like an old fool.'

'My dear mother. I am really at a loss to understand what you mean.'

Esa replied composedly:

'You always were a fool, Imhotep.'

Imhotep drew himself up and spluttered angrily. Though usually comfortably conscious of his own importance, his mother could always pierce the armour of his self-esteem. In her presence he felt himself dwindling. The faint sarcastic gleam of her nearly sightless eyes never failed to disconcert him. His mother, there was no denying, had never had an exaggerated opinion of his capabilities. And although he knew well that his own estimate of himself was the true one and his mother's a maternal idiosyncrasy of no importance—yet her attitude never failed to puncture his happy conceit of himself.

'Is it so unusual for a man to bring home a concubine?'

'Not at all unusual. Men are usually fools.'

'I fail to see where the folly comes in.'

'Do you imagine that the presence of this girl is going to make for harmony in the household? Satipy and Kait will be beside themselves and will inflame their husbands.'

'What has it to do with them? What right have they to object?'

'None.'

Imhotep began to walk up and down angrily.

'Can I not do as I please in my own house? Do I not support my sons and their wives? Do they not owe the very bread they eat to me? Do I not tell them so without ceasing?'

'You are too fond of saying so, Imhotep.'

'It is the truth. They all depend on me. All of them!'

'And are you sure that this is a good thing?'

'Are you saying that it is not a good thing for a man to support his family?'

Esa sighed.

'They work for you, remember.'

'Do you want me to encourage them in idleness? Naturally they work.'

'They are grown men—at least Yahmose and Sobek are—more than grown.'

'Sobek has no judgement. He does everything wrong. Also he is frequently impertinent which I will not tolerate. Yahmose is a good obedient boy—'

'A good deal more than a boy!'

'But sometimes I have to tell him things two or three times before he takes them in. I have to think of everything—be everywhere! All the time I am away, I am dictating to scribes—writing full instructions so that my sons can carry them out . . . I hardly rest—I hardly sleep! And now when I come home, having earned a little peace, there is to be fresh difficulty! Even you, my mother, deny my right to have a concubine like other men—you are angry—'

Esa interrupted him.

'I am not angry. I am amused. There will be good sport to watch in the household—but I say all the same that when you go North again you had best take the girl with you.'

'Her place is here, in my household! And woe to any who dare ill-treat her.'

'It is not a question of ill-treatment. But remember, it is easy to kindle a fire in dry stubble. It has been said of women that "the place where they are is not good . . ."'

Esa paused and said slowly:

'Nofret is beautiful. But remember this: *Men are made fools by the gleaming limbs of women, and lo, in a minute they are become discoloured cornelians . . .*'

Her voice deepened as she quoted:

'A trifle, a little, the likeness of a dream, and death comes as the end . . .'

CHAPTER 4

Third Month of Inundation 15th Day

Imhotep listened to Sobek's explanation of the sale of the timber in ominous silence. His face had grown very red and a small pulse was beating in his temple.

Sobek's air of easy nonchalance wore a little thin. He had intended to carry things off with a high hand, but in the face of his father's gathering frowns, he found himself stammering and hesitating.

Imhotep finally cut him short impatiently.

'Yes, yes, yes—you thought that you knew more than I did—you departed from my instructions—it is always the same—unless I am here to see to everything . . .' He sighed. 'What would become of you boys without me I cannot imagine!'

Sobek went on doggedly:

'There was a chance of making a much bigger profit— I took the risk. One cannot always be pettifogging and cautious!'

'There is nothing cautious about you, Sobek! You are rash and much too bold and your judgement is always wrong.'

39

Agatha Christie

'Do I ever have a chance to exercise my judgement?'

Imhotep said dryly:

'You have done so this time—and against my express orders—'

'*Orders?* Have I always got to take orders? I am a grown man.'

Losing control of his temper, Imhotep shouted:

'Who feeds you, who clothes you? Who thinks of the future? Who has your welfare—the welfare of all of you—constantly in mind? When the river was low and we were threatened with famine, did I not arrange for food to be sent South to you? You are lucky to have such a father—who thinks of everything! And what do I ask in return? Only that you should work hard, do your best, and obey the instructions I send you—'

'Yes,' shouted Sobek. 'We are to work for you like slaves—so that you can buy gold and jewels for your concubine!'

Imhotep advanced towards him, bristling with rage.

'Insolent boy—to speak like that to your father. Be careful or I will say that this is no longer your home—and you can go elsewhere!'

'And if *you* are not careful I *will* go! I have ideas, I tell you—good ideas—that would bring in wealth if I was not tied down by pettifogging caution and never allowed to act as I choose.'

'Have you finished?'

Imhotep's tone was ominous. Sobek, a trifle deflated, muttered angrily:

'Yes—yes—I have no more to say—*now*.'

'Then go and see after the cattle. This is no time for idling.'

40

Sobek turned and strode angrily away. Nofret was standing not far away and as he passed her she looked sideways at him and laughed. At her laugh the blood came up in Sobek's face—he made an angry half step towards her. She stood quite still, looking at him out of contemptuous half-closed eyes.

Sobek muttered something and resumed his former direction. Nofret laughed again, then walked slowly on to where Imhotep was now turning his attention to Yahmose.

'What possessed you to let Sobek act in that foolish fashion?' he demanded irritably. 'You should have prevented it! Don't you know by now that he has no judgement in buying and selling? He thinks everything will turn out as he wants it to turn out.'

Yahmose said apologetically:

'You do not realize my difficulties, father. You told me to entrust Sobek with the sale of the timber. It was necessary therefore that it should be left to him to use his judgement.'

'Judgement? Judgement? He has no judgement! He is to do what I instruct him to do—and it is for *you* to see that he does exactly that.'

Yahmose flushed.

'I? What authority have *I*?'

'What authority? The authority I give you.'

'But I have no real status. If I were legally associated with you—'

He broke off as Nofret came up. She was yawning and twisting a scarlet poppy in her hands.

'Won't you come to the little pavilion by the lake, Imhotep?

It is cool there and there is fruit waiting for you and Keda beer. Surely you have finished giving your orders by now.'

'In a minute, Nofret—in a minute.'

Nofret said in a soft, deep voice:

'Come *now*. I want you to come now . . .'

Imhotep looked pleased and a little sheepish. Yahmose said quickly before his father could speak:

'Let us just speak of this first. It is important. I want to ask you—'

Nofret spoke directly to Imhotep, turning her shoulder on Yahmose:

'Can you not do what you want in your own house?'

Imhotep said sharply to Yahmose:

'Another time, my son. Another time.'

He went with Nofret and Yahmose stood on the porch looking after them.

Satipy came out from the house and joined him.

'Well,' she demanded eagerly, 'have you spoken to him? What did he say?'

Yahmose sighed.

'Do not be so impatient, Satipy. The time was not—propitious.'

Satipy gave an angry exclamation.

'Oh yes—that is what you *would* say! That is what you will always say! The truth is you are *afraid* of your father—you are as timid as a sheep—you bleat at him—you will not stand up to him like a man! Do you not recall the things you promised me? I tell you *I* am the better man of us two! You promise—you say: "I will ask my father—at once—the very first day." And what happens—'

Satipy paused—for breath, not because she had finished—but Yahmose cut in mildly:

'You are wrong, Satipy. I began to speak—but we were interrupted.'

'Interrupted? By whom?'

'By Nofret.'

'Nofret! That woman! Your father should not let his concubine interrupt when he is speaking of business to his eldest son. Women should not concern themselves with business.'

Possibly Yahmose wished that Satipy herself would live up to the maxim she was enunciating so glibly, but he was given no opportunity to speak. His wife swept on:

'Your father should have made that clear to her at once.'

'My father,' said Yahmose drily, 'showed no signs of displeasure.'

'It is disgraceful,' Satipy declared. 'Your father is completely bewitched by her. He lets her say and do as she pleases.'

Yahmose said thoughtfully:

'She is very beautiful . . .'

Satipy snorted.

'Oh, she has looks of a kind. But no manners! No upbringing! She does not care how rude she is to all of us.'

'Perhaps *you* are rude to her?'

'I am the soul of politeness. Kait and I treat her with every courtesy. Oh, she shall have nothing of which to go complaining to your father. We can wait our time, Kait and I.'

Yahmose looked up sharply.

'How do you mean—*wait your time*?'

Satipy laughed meaningfully as she moved away.

'My meaning is woman's meaning—you would not understand. We have our ways—and our weapons! Nofret would do well to moderate her insolence. What does a woman's life come to in the end, after all? It is spent in the back of the house—amongst the other women.'

There was a peculiar significance in Satipy's tone. She added:

'Your father will not always be here . . . He will go away again to his estates in the North. And then—we shall see.'

'Satipy—'

Satipy laughed—a hard-sounding, high laugh, and went back into the house.

By the lake the children were running about and playing. Yahmose's two boys were fine, handsome little fellows, looking more like Satipy than like their father. Then there were Sobek's three—the youngest a mere toddling baby. And there was Teti, a grave, handsome child of four years old.

They laughed and shouted, threw balls—occasionally a dispute broke out and a childish wail of anger rose high and shrill.

Sitting sipping his beer, with Nofret beside him, Imhotep murmured: 'How fond children are of playing by water. It was always so, I remember. But, by Hathor, what a noise they make!'

Nofret said quickly:

'Yes—and it could be so peaceful . . . Why do you not

tell them to go away whilst you are here? After all when the master of the house wants relaxation a proper respect should be shown. Don't you agree?'

'I—well—' Imhotep hesitated. The idea was new to him but pleasing. 'I do not really mind them,' he finished, doubtfully.

He added rather weakly:

'They are accustomed to play here always as they please.'

'When you are away, yes,' said Nofret quickly. 'But I think, Imhotep, considering all that you do for your family, they should show more sense of your dignity—of your importance. You are too gentle—too easygoing.'

Imhotep sighed placidly.

'It has always been my failing. I never insist on the outward forms.'

'And therefore these women, your son's wives, take advantage of your kindness. It should be understood that when you come here for repose, there must be silence and tranquillity. See, I will go and tell Kait to take her children away and the others too. Then you shall have peace and contentment here.'

'You are a thoughtful girl, Nofret—yes, a good girl. You are always thinking of my comfort.'

Nofret murmured: 'Your pleasure is mine.'

She got up and went to where Kait was kneeling by the water playing with a little model barge which her second child, a rather spoilt-looking-boy, was trying to float.

Nofret said curtly:

'Will you take the children away, Kait?'

Kait stared up at her uncomprehendingly.

45

Agatha Christie

'Away? What do you mean? This is where they always play.'

'Not today. Imhotep wants peace. These children of yours are noisy.'

Colour flamed into Kait's heavy face.

'You should mend your ways of speech, Nofret! Imhotep likes to see his sons' children playing here. He has said so.'

'Not today,' said Nofret. 'He has sent me to tell you to take the whole noisy brood into the house, so that he can sit in peace—with me.'

'With *you* . . .' Kait stopped abruptly in what she had been about to say. Then she got up and walked to where Imhotep was half-sitting, half-lying. Nofret followed her.

Kait spoke without circumlocution.

'Your concubine says I am to take the children away from here? Why? What are they doing that is wrong? For what reason should they be banished?'

'I should have thought the wish of the master of the house was enough,' said Nofret softly.

'Exactly—exactly,' said Imhotep pettishly. 'Why should I have to give *reasons*? Whose house is this?'

'I suppose it is *she* who wants them away.' Kait turned and looked Nofret up and down.

'Nofret thinks of my comfort—of my enjoyment,' said Imhotep. 'No one else in this house ever considers it—except perhaps poor Henet.'

'So the children are not to play here any more?'

'Not when I have come here to rest.'

Kait's anger flamed forth suddenly:

'Why do you let this woman turn you against your

46

own blood? Why should she come and interfere with the ways of the house? With what has always been done.'

Imhotep suddenly began to shout. He felt a need to vindicate himself.

'It is *I* who say what is to be done here—not you! You are all in league to do as you choose—to arrange everything to suit yourselves. And when I, the master of the house, come home, no proper attention is paid to my wishes. But I *am* master here, let me tell you! I am constantly planning and working for your welfare—but am I given gratitude, are my wishes respected? No. First, Sobek is insolent and disrespectful, and now you, Kait, try to browbeat me! What am I supporting you all for? Take care—or I shall cease to support you. Sobek talks of going—then let him go and take you and your children with him.'

For a moment Kait stood perfectly still. There was no expression at all on her heavy, rather vacant face. Then she said in a voice from which all emotion had been eliminated:

'I will take the children into the house . . .'

She moved a step or two, pausing by Nofret. In a low voice Kait said:

'This is *your* doing, Nofret. I shall not forget. No, I shall not forget . . .'

CHAPTER 5

Fourth Month of Inundation 5th Day

Imhotep breathed a sigh of satisfaction as he finished his ceremonial duties as Mortuary Priest. The ritual had been observed with meticulous detail—for Imhotep was in every respect a most conscientious man. He had poured the libations, burnt incense, and offered the customary offerings of food and drink.

Now, in the cool shade of the adjacent rock chamber where Hori was waiting for him, Imhotep became once more the land-owner and the man of affairs. Together the two men discussed business matters, prevailing prices, and the profits resulting from crops, cattle, and timber.

After half an hour or so, Imhotep nodded his head with satisfaction.

'You have an excellent head for business, Hori,' he said.

The other smiled.

'I should have, Imhotep. I have been your man of affairs for many years now.'

'And a most faithful one. Now, I have a matter to discuss

with you. It concerns Ipy. He complains that his position is subordinate.'

'He is still very young.'

'But he shows great ability. He feels that his brothers are not always fair to him. Sobek, it seems, is rough and over-bearing—and Yahmose's continual caution and timidity irk him. Ipy is high-spirited. He does not like taking orders. Moreover he says that it is only I, his father, who have the right to command.'

'That is true,' said Hori. 'And it has struck me, Imhotep, that that is a weakness here on the estate. May I speak freely?'

'Certainly, my good Hori. Your words are always thoughtful and well considered.'

'Then I say this. When you are away, Imhotep, there should be someone here who has real authority.'

'I trust my affairs to you and to Yahmose—'

'I know that we act for you in your absence—but that is not enough. Why not appoint one of your sons as a partner—associate him with you by a legal deed of settlement?'

Imhotep paced up and down frowning.

'Which of my sons do you suggest? Sobek has an authoritative manner—but he is insubordinate—I could not trust him. His disposition is not good.'

'I was thinking of Yahmose. He is your eldest son. He has a gentle and affectionate disposition. He is devoted to you.'

'Yes, he has a good disposition—but he is too timid—too yielding. He gives in to everybody. Now if Ipy were only a little older—'

Agatha Christie

Hori said quickly:

'It is dangerous to give power to too young a man.'

'True—true—well, Hori, I will think of what you have said. Yahmose is certainly a good son . . . an obedient son . . .'

Hori said gently but urgently:

'You would, I think, be wise.'

Imhotep looked at him curiously.

'What is in your mind, Hori?'

Hori said slowly:

'I said just now that it is dangerous to give a man power when he is too young. But it is also dangerous to give it to him too late.'

'You mean that he has become too used to obeying orders and not to giving them. Well, perhaps there is something in that.'

Imhotep sighed.

'It is a difficult task to rule a family! The women in particular are hard to manage. Satipy has an ungovernable temper, Kait is often sulky. But I have made it clear to them that Nofret is to be treated in a proper fashion. I think I may say that—'

He broke off. A slave was coming panting up the narrow pathway.

'What is this?'

'Master—a barge is here. A scribe called Kameni has come with a message from Memphis.'

Imhotep got up fussily.

'More trouble,' he exclaimed. 'As sure as Ra sails the Heavens this will be more trouble! Unless I am on hand to attend to things everything goes wrong.'

He went stamping down the path and Hori sat quite still looking after him.

There was a troubled expression on his face.

Renisenb had been wandering aimlessly along the bank of the Nile when she heard shouts and commotion and saw people running towards the landing stage.

She ran and joined them. In the boat that was pulling to shore stood a young man, and just for a moment, as she saw him outlined against the bright light, her heart missed a beat.

A mad, fantastic thought leapt into her mind.

'It is Khay,' she thought. 'Khay returned from the Underworld.'

Then she mocked herself for the superstitious fancy. Because in her own remembrance, she always thought of Khay as sailing on the Nile, and this was indeed a young man of about Khay's build—she had imagined a fantasy. This man was younger than Khay, with an easy, supple grace, and had a laughing, gay face.

He had come, he told them, from Imhotep's estates in the North. He was a scribe and his name was Kameni.

A slave was despatched for her father and Kameni was taken to the house where food and drink were put before him. Presently her father arrived and there was much consultation and talking.

The gist of it all filtered through into the women's quarters with Henet, as usual, as the purveyor of the news. Renisenb sometimes wondered how it was that Henet always contrived to know all about everything.

Kameni, it seemed, was a young scribe in Imhotep's employ—the son of one of Imhotep's cousins. Kameni had discovered certain fraudulent dispositions—a falsifying of the accounts, and since the matter had many ramifications and involved the stewards of the property, he had thought it best to come South in person and report.

Renisenb was not much interested. It was clever, she thought, of Kameni to have discovered all this. Her father would be pleased with him.

The immediate outcome of the matter was that Imhotep made hurried preparations for departure. He had not meant to leave for another two months, but now the sooner he was on the spot the better.

The whole household was summoned and innumerable exordiums and recommendations were made. This was to be done and that. Yahmose was on no account to do such and such a thing. Sobek was to exercise the utmost discretion over something else. It was all, Renisenb thought, very familiar. Yahmose was attentive, Sobek was sulky. Hori, as usual, was calm and efficient. Ipy's demands and importunities were put aside with more sharpness than usual.

'You are too young to have a separate allowance. Obey Yahmose. He knows my wishes and commands.' Imhotep placed a hand on his eldest son's shoulder. 'I trust you, Yahmose. When I return we will speak once more of a partnership.'

Yahmose flushed quickly with pleasure. He drew himself a little more erect.

Imhotep went on:

'See only that all goes well in my absence. See to it that

52

my concubine is well treated—and with due honour and respect. She is in your charge. It is for you to control the conduct of the women of the household. See that Satipy curbs her tongue. See also that Sobek duly instructs Kait. Renisenb, also, must act towards Nofret with courtesy. Then I will have no unkindness shown toward our good Henet. The women, I know, find her tiresome sometimes. She has been here long and thinks herself privileged to say many things that are sometimes unwelcome. She has, I know, neither beauty nor wit—but she is faithful, remember, and has always been devoted to my interests. I will not have her despised and abused.'

'Everything shall be done as you say,' said Yahmose. 'But Henet sometimes makes trouble with her tongue.'

'Pah! Nonsense! All women do. Not Henet more than another. Now as to Kameni, he shall remain here. We can do with another scribe and he can assist Hori. As for that land that we have rented to the woman Yaii—'

Imhotep went off into meticulous details.

When at last all was ready for the departure Imhotep felt a sudden qualm. He took Nofret aside and said doubtfully:

'Nofret, are you content to remain here? Would it be, perhaps, best if, after all, you came with me?'

Nofret shook her head and smiled.

'You will not be long absent,' she said.

'Three months—perhaps four. Who knows?'

'You see—it will not be long. I shall be content here.'

Imhotep said fussily:

'I have enjoined upon Yahmose—upon all my sons—that

you are to have every consideration. On their heads be it if you have anything of which to complain!'

'They will do as you say, I am sure, Imhotep.' Nofret paused. Then she said, 'Who is there here whom I can trust absolutely? Someone who is truly devoted to your interests? I do not mean one of the family.'

'Hori—my good Hori? He is in every way my right hand—and a man of good sense and discrimination.'

Nofret said slowly:

'He and Yahmose are like brothers. Perhaps—'

'There is Kameni. He, too, is a scribe. I will enjoin on him to place himself at your service. If you have anything of which to complain, he will write down your words with his pen and despatch the complaint to me.'

Nofret nodded appreciatively.

'That is a good thought. Kameni comes from the North. He knows my father. He will not be influenced by family considerations.'

'And Henet,' exclaimed Imhotep. 'There is Henet.'

'Yes,' said Nofret, reflectively. 'There is Henet. Suppose that you were to speak to her now—in front of me?'

'An excellent plan.'

Henet was sent for and came with her usual cringing eagerness. She was full of lamentations over Imhotep's departure. Imhotep cut her short with abruptness.

'Yes, yes, my good Henet—but these things must be. I am a man who can seldom count on any stretch of peace or rest. I must toil ceaselessly for my family—little though they sometimes appreciate it. Now I wish to speak to you very seriously. You love me faithfully and devotedly, I know—I can leave you in a position of trust. Guard Nofret here—she is very dear to me.'

'Whoever is dear to you, master, is dear to me,' Henet declared with fervour.

'Very good. Then you will devote yourself to Nofret's interests?'

Henet turned towards Nofret who was watching her under lowered lids.

'You are too beautiful, Nofret,' she said. 'That is the trouble. That is why the others are jealous—but *I* will look after you—I will warn you of all they say and do. You can count on me!'

There was a pause whilst the eyes of the two women met.

'You can count on me,' Henet repeated.

A slow smile came to Nofret's lips—a rather curious smile.

'Yes,' she said. 'I understand you, Henet. I think I can count on you.'

Imhotep cleared his throat noisily.

'Then I think all is arranged—yes—everything is satisfactory. Organization—that has always been my strong point.'

There was a dry cackle of laughter and Imhotep turned sharply to see his mother standing in the entrance of the room. She was supporting her weight on a stick and looked more dried up and malevolent than ever.

'What a wonderful son I have!' she observed.

'I must not delay—there are some instructions to Hori—' Muttering importantly, Imhotep hurried from the room. He managed to avoid meeting his mother's eye.

Esa gave an imperious nod of the head to Henet—and Henet glided obediently out of the room.

Nofret had risen. She and Esa stood looking at each other. Esa said: 'So my son is leaving you behind? You had better go with him, Nofret.'

'He wishes me to stay here.'

Nofret's voice was soft and submissive. Esa gave a shrill chuckle.

'Little good that would be if you wanted to go! And why do you not want to go? I do not understand you. What is there for you here? You are a girl who has lived in cities—who has perhaps travelled. Why do you choose the monotony of day after day here—amongst those who—I am frank—do not like you—who in fact dislike you?'

'So you dislike me?'

Esa shook her head.

'No—I do not dislike you. I am old and though I can see but dimly—I can still see beauty and enjoy it. You are beautiful, Nofret, and the sight of you pleases my old eyes. Because of your beauty I wish you well. I am warning you. Go North with my son.'

Again Nofret repeated: 'He wishes me to stay here.'

The submissive tone was now definitely impregnated with mockery. Esa said sharply:

'You have a purpose in remaining here. What is it, I wonder? Very well, on your own head be it. But be careful. Act discreetly. And trust no one.'

She wheeled abruptly and went out. Nofret stood quite still. Very slowly her lips curved upwards in a wide, catlike smile.

PART TWO

Winter

CHAPTER 6

First Month of Winter 4th Day

Renisenb had got into the habit of going up to the Tomb almost every day. Sometimes Yahmose and Hori would be there together, sometimes Hori alone, sometimes there would be no one—but always Renisenb was aware of a curious relief and peace—a feeling almost of escape. She liked it best when Hori was there alone. There was something in his gravity, his incurious acceptance of her coming, that gave her a strange feeling of contentment. She would sit in the shade of the rock chamber entrance with one knee raised and her hands clasped round it, and stare out over the green belt of cultivation to where the Nile showed a pale gleaming blue and beyond it to a distance of pale soft fawns and creams and pinks, all melting hazily into each other.

She had come the first time, months ago now, on a sudden wish to escape from a world of intense femininity. She wanted stillness and companionship—and she had found them here. The wish to escape was still with her, but it was no longer a mere revulsion from the stress and fret of domesticity. It was something more definite, more alarming.

She said to Hori one day: 'I am afraid . . .'

'Why are you afraid, Renisenb?' He studied her gravely.

Renisenb took a minute or two to think. Then she said slowly:

'Do you remember saying to me once that there were two evils—one that came from without and one from within?'

'Yes, I remember.'

'You were speaking, so you said afterwards, about diseases that attack fruit and crops, but I have been thinking—it is the same with *people*.'

Hori nodded slowly.

'So you have found that out . . . Yes, you are right, Renisenb.'

Renisenb said abruptly:

'It is happening now—down there at the house. Evil has come—from outside! And I know who has brought it. It is Nofret.'

Hori said slowly:

'You think so?'

Renisenb nodded vigorously.

'Yes, yes, I know what I am talking about. Listen, Hori, when I came up to you here and said that everything was the same even to Satipy and Kait quarrelling—that was true. But those quarrels, Hori, were not *real* quarrels. I mean Satipy and Kait *enjoyed* them—they made the time pass—neither of the women felt any real anger against each other! But now it is different. Now they do not just say

60

things that are rude and unpleasant—they say things that they mean shall *hurt*—and when they have seen that a thing hurts then they are glad! It is horrid, Hori—horrid! Yesterday Satipy was so angry that she ran a long gold pin into Kait's arm—and a day or two ago Kait dropped a heavy copper pan full of boiling fat over Satipy's foot. And it is the same everywhere—Satipy rails at Yahmose far into the night—we can all hear her. Yahmose looks sick and tired and hunted. And Sobek goes off to the village and stays there with women and comes back drunk and shouts and boasts and says how clever he is!'

'Some of these things are true, I know,' said Hori, slowly. 'But why should you blame Nofret?'

'Because it is her doing! It is always the things she says—little things—clever things—that start it all. She is like the goad with which you prick oxen. She is clever, too, in knowing just *what* to say. Sometimes I think it is Henet who tells her . . .'

'Yes,' said Hori thoughtfully. 'That might well be.'

Renisenb shivered.

'I don't like Henet. I hate the way she creeps about. She is so devoted to us all, and yet none of us want her devotion. How *could* my mother have brought her here and been so fond of her?'

'We have only Henet's word for that,' said Hori drily.

'Why should Henet be so fond of Nofret and follow her round and whisper and fawn upon her? Oh, Hori, I tell you I am *afraid*! I hate Nofret! I wish she would go away. She is beautiful and cruel and *bad*!'

'What a child you are, Renisenb.'

Then Hori added quietly:

'Nofret is coming up here now.'

Renisenb turned her head. Together they watched Nofret come slowly up the steep path that led up the cliff face. She was smiling to herself and humming a little tune under her breath.

When she reached the place where they were, she looked round her and smiled. It was a smile of amused curiosity. 'So this is where you slip away to every day, Renisenb.'

Renisenb did not answer. She had the angry, defeated feeling of a child whose refuge has been discovered.

Nofret looked about her again.

'And this is the famous Tomb?'

'As you say, Nofret,' said Hori.

She looked at him, her cat-like mouth curving into a smile.

'I've no doubt you find it profitable, Hori. You are a good man of business, so I hear.'

There was a tinge of malice in her voice, but Hori remained unmoved, smiling his quiet, grave smile.

'It is profitable to all of us ... Death is always profitable ...'

Nofret gave a quick shiver as she looked round her, her eyes sweeping over the offering tables, the entrance to the shrine and the false door.

She cried sharply:

'I hate Death!'

'You should not.' Hori's tone was quiet. 'Death is the chief source of wealth here in Egypt. Death bought the jewels you wear, Nofret. Death feeds you and clothes you.'

She stared at him.

'What do you mean?'

'I mean that Imhotep is a ka-priest—a mortuary priest—all his lands, all his cattle, his timber, his flax, his barley, are the endowment of a Tomb.'

He paused and then went on reflectively:

'We are a strange people, we Egyptians. We love life—and so we start very early to plan for death. That is where the wealth of Egypt goes—into pyramids, into tombs, into tomb endowment.'

Nofret said violently:

'*Will* you stop talking about death, Hori! I do not like it!'

'Because you are truly Egyptian—because you love life, because—sometimes—you feel the shadow of death very near . . .'

'Stop!'

She turned on him violently. Then, shrugging her shoulders, she turned away and began to descend the path.

Renisenb breathed a sigh of satisfaction.

'I am glad she has gone,' she said childishly. 'You frightened her, Hori.'

'Yes . . . Did I frighten you, Renisenb?'

'N-no.' Renisenb sounded a little unsure. 'It is true what you said, only I had never thought of it that way before. My father *is* a mortuary priest.'

Hori said with sudden bitterness:

'All Egypt is obsessed by death! And do you know why, Renisenb? Because we have eyes in our bodies, but none in our minds. We cannot conceive of a life other than this one—of a life after death. We can visualize only a continuation of what we know. We have no real belief in a God.'

Renisenb stared at him in amazement.

'How can you say that, Hori? Why, we have many, *many* Gods—so many that I could not name them all. Only last night we were saying, all of us, which Gods we preferred. Sobek was all for Sakhmet and Kait prays always to Meskhant. Kameni swears by Thoth as is natural, being a scribe. Satipy is for the falcon-headed Horus and also for our own Mereseer. Yahmose says that Ptah is to be worshipped because he made all things. I myself love Isis. And Henet is all for our local God Amün. She says that there are prophecies amongst the priests that one day Amün will be the greatest God in all Egypt—so she takes him offerings now while he is still a small God. And there is Rē, the Sun God, and Osiris before whom the hearts of the dead are weighed.'

Renisenb paused, out of breath. Hori was smiling at her.

'And what is the difference, Renisenb, between a God and a man?'

She stared at him.

'The Gods are—they are *magic*!'

'That is all?'

'I don't know what you mean, Hori.'

'I meant that to you a God is only a man or a woman who can do certain things that men and women cannot do.'

'You say such odd things! I cannot understand you.'

She looked at him with a puzzled face—then glancing down over the valley, her attention was caught by something else.

'Look,' she exclaimed. 'Nofret is talking to Sobek. She is laughing. Oh!—' she gave a sudden gasp, 'no, it is nothing.

I thought he was going to strike her. She is going back to the house and he is coming up here.'

Sobek arrived looking like a thundercloud.

'May a crocodile devour that woman!' he cried. 'My father was more of a fool than usual when he took her for a concubine!'

'What did she say to you?' asked Hori curiously.

'She insulted me as usual! Asked if my father had entrusted me with the sale of any more timber. Her tongue stings like a serpent. I would like to kill her.'

He moved along the platform and, picking up a piece of rock, threw it down to the valley below. The sound of it bouncing off the cliff seemed to please him. He levered up a larger piece, then sprang back as a snake that had been coiled up beneath it raised its head. It reared up, hissing, and Renisenb saw that it was a cobra.

Catching up a heavy staff Sobek attacked it furiously. A well directed blow broke its back, but Sobek continued to slash at it, his head thrown back, his eyes sparkling, and below his breath he muttered some word which Renisenb only half heard and did not recognize.

She cried out: 'Stop, Sobek, stop—it's dead!'

Sobek paused, then he threw the staff away and laughed.

'One poisonous snake the less in the world.'

He laughed again, his good humour restored, and clattered off down the path again.

Renisenb said in a low voice: 'I believe Sobek—*likes* killing things!'

'Yes.'

There was no surprise in the word. Hori was merely

acknowledging a fact which he evidently already knew well. Renisenb turned to stare at him. She said slowly:

'Snakes are dangerous—but how beautiful that cobra looked . . .'

She stared down at its broken, twisted body. For some unknown reason she felt a pang at her heart.

Hori said dreamily:

'I remember when we were all small children—Sobek attacked Yahmose. Yahmose was a year older, but Sobek was the bigger and stronger. He had a stone and he was banging Yahmose's head with it. Your mother came running and tore them apart. I remember how she stood looking down at Yahmose—and how she cried out: "You must not do things like that, Sobek—it is dangerous! I tell you, it is *dangerous*!"' He paused and went on, 'She was very beautiful . . . I thought so as a child. You are like her, Renisenb.'

'Am I?' Renisenb felt pleased—warmed. Then she asked:

'Was Yahmose badly hurt?'

'No, it was not as bad as it looked. Sobek was very ill the next day. It might have been something he ate, but your mother said it was his rage and the hot sun—it was the middle of summer.'

'Sobek has a terrible temper,' said Renisenb thoughtfully.

She looked again at the dead snake and turned away with a shiver.

When Renisenb got back to the house Kameni was sitting on the front porch with a roll of papyrus. He was singing and she paused a minute and listened to the words.

'*I will go to Memphis*,' sang Kameni, '*I will go to Ptah, Lord of Truth. I will say to Ptah, "Give me my sister tonight." The stream is wine, Ptah is its reeds, Sekhmet its lotus, Earit its bud, Nefertum its flower. I will say to Ptah, "Give me my sister tonight. The dawn breaks through her beauty. Memphis is a dish of love apples set before the fair face . . ."*'

He looked up and smiled at Renisenb.

'Do you like my song, Renisenb?'

'What is it?'

'It is a love song from Memphis.'

He kept his eyes on her, singing softly:

'*Her arms are full of branches of the persea, her hair is weighed down with unguent. She is like a Princess of the Lord of the Two Lands.*'

The colour came up in Renisenb's face. She passed on quickly into the house and almost collided with Nofret.

'Why are you in such a hurry, Renisenb?'

Nofret's voice had a sharp edge to it. Renisenb looked at her in faint surprise. Nofret was not smiling. Her face looked grim and tense and Renisenb noticed that her hands were clenched at her sides.

'I am sorry, Nofret, I did not see you. It is dark in here when you come from the light outside.'

'Yes, it is dark here . . .' Nofret paused a moment. 'It would be pleasanter outside—on the porch—with Kameni's singing to listen to. He sings well, does he not?'

'Yes—yes, I am sure he does.'

'Yet you did not stay to listen? Kameni will be disappointed.'

Agatha Christie

Renisenb's cheeks felt hot again. Nofret's cold, sneering glance made her uncomfortable.

'Do you not like love songs, Renisenb?'

'Does it matter to you, Nofret, what I like and do not like?'

'So little cats have claws.'

'What do you mean?'

Nofret laughed. 'You are not such a fool as you look, Renisenb. So you find Kameni handsome? Well, that will please him no doubt.'

'I think you are quite odious,' said Renisenb passionately.

She ran past Nofret towards the back of the house. She heard the girl's mocking laugh. But through that laugh, sounding clearly in her memory, was the echo of Kameni's voice and the song that he had sung with his eyes watching her face . . .

That night Renisenb had a dream.

She was with Khay, sailing with him in the Barque of the Dead in the Underworld. Khay was standing in the bows of the boat—she could only see the back of his head. Then, as they drew near to sunrise, Khay turned his head, and Renisenb saw that it was not Khay but Kameni. And at the same time the prow of the barque, the serpent's head, began to writhe. It was a live serpent, a cobra, and Renisenb thought: *'It is the serpent that comes out in the Tombs to eat the souls of the dead.'* She was paralysed with fear. And then she saw the serpent's face was the face of Nofret and she woke up screaming: 'Nofret—Nofret . . .'

She had not really screamed—it was all in the dream. She lay still, her heart beating, telling herself that none of all this was real. And then she thought suddenly: 'That is what Sobek said when he was killing the snake yesterday. He said: *"Nofret"* . . .'

CHAPTER 7

First Month of Winter 5th Day

Renisenb's dream had left her wakeful. She slept after it only in snatches and towards morning she did not sleep at all. She was obsessed by an obscure feeling of impending evil.

She rose early and went out of the house. Her steps led her, as they did so often, to the Nile. There were fishermen out already and a big barge rowing with powerful strokes towards Thebes. There were other boats with sails flapping in the faint puffs of wind.

Something turned over in Renisenb's heart, the stirring of a desire for something she could not name. She thought, 'I feel—I feel—' But she did not know what it was that she felt! That is to say, she knew no words to fit the sensation. She thought, 'I want—but what do I want?'

Was it Khay she wanted? Khay was dead—he would not come back. She said to herself, 'I shall not think of Khay any more. What is the use? It is over, all that.'

Then she noticed another figure standing looking after the barge that was making for Thebes—and something about that figure—some emotion it expressed by its very motionlessness struck Renisenb, even as she recognized Nofret.

Nofret staring out at the Nile. Nofret—alone. Nofret thinking of—what?

With a little shock Renisenb suddenly realized how little they all knew about Nofret. They had accepted her as an enemy—a stranger—without interest or curiosity in her life or the surroundings from which she had come.

It must, Renisenb thought suddenly, be sad for Nofret alone here, without friends, surrounded only by people who disliked her.

Slowly Renisenb went forward until she was standing by Nofret's side. Nofret turned her head for a moment then moved it back again and resumed her study of the Nile. Her face was expressionless.

Renisenb said timidly:

'There are a lot of boats on the river.'

'Yes.'

Renisenb went on, obeying some obscure impulse towards friendliness:

'Is it like this, at all, where you come from?'

Nofret laughed, a short, rather bitter laugh.

'No, indeed. My father is a merchant in Memphis. It is gay and amusing in Memphis. There is music and singing and dancing. Then my father travels a good deal. I have been with him to Syria—to Byblos beyond the Gazelle's Nose. I have been with him in a big ship on the wide seas.'

She spoke with pride and animation.

Renisenb stood quite still, her mind working slowly, but with growing interest and understanding.

'It must be very dull for you here,' she said slowly.

Nofret laughed impatiently.

'It is dead here—dead—nothing but ploughing and sowing and reaping and grazing—and talk of crops—and wranglings about the price of flax.'

Renisenb was still wrestling with unfamiliar thoughts as she watched Nofret sideways.

And suddenly, as though it was something physical, a great wave of anger and misery and despair seemed to emanate from the girl at her side.

Renisenb thought: 'She is as young as I am—younger. And she is the concubine of that old man, that fussy, kindly, but rather ridiculous old man, my father . . .'

What did she, Renisenb, know about Nofret? Nothing at all. What was it Hori had said yesterday when she had cried out, 'She is beautiful and cruel and bad!'

'You are a child, Renisenb.' That was what he had said. Renisenb knew now what he meant. Those words of hers had meant nothing—you could not dismiss a human being so easily. What sorrow, what bitterness, what despair lay behind Nofret's cruel smile? What had Renisenb, what had any of them, done to make Nofret welcome?

Renisenb said stumblingly, childishly:

'You hate us all—I see why—we have not been kind—but now—it is not too late. Can we not, you and I, Nofret, can we not be sisters to each other? You are far away from all you know—you are alone—can I not help?'

Her words faltered into silence. Nofret turned slowly.

For a minute or two her face was expressionless—there was even, Renisenb thought, a momentary softening in her eyes. In that early morning stillness, with its strange clarity and peace, it was as though Nofret hesitated—as though Renisenb's words had touched in her some last core of irresolution.

It was a strange moment, a moment Renisenb was to remember afterwards . . .

Then, gradually, Nofret's expression changed. It became heavily malevolent, her eyes smouldered. Before the fury of hate and malice in her glance, Renisenb recoiled a step.

Nofret said in a low, fierce voice:

'Go! I want nothing from any of you. Stupid fools, that is what you all are, every one of you . . .'

She paused a moment, then wheeled round and retraced her steps towards the house, walking with energy.

Renisenb followed her slowly. Curiously enough, Nofret's words had not made her angry. They had opened before her eyes a black abyss of hate and misery—something quite unknown as yet in her own experience, and in her mind was only a confused, groping thought of how dreadful it must be to feel like that.

As Nofret entered the gateway and crossed the courtyard, one of Kait's children came running across her path, chasing a ball.

Nofret thrust the child out of her way with an angry thrust that sent the little girl sprawling on the ground. The child set up a wail and Renisenb ran to her and picked her up, saying indignantly:

'You should not have done that, Nofret! You have hurt her, see. She has cut her chin.'

Nofret laughed stridently.

'So I should be careful not to hurt these spoiled brats? Why? Are their mothers so careful of *my* feelings?'

Kait had come running out of the house at the sound of her child's wails. She ran to it, examining the injured face. Then she turned on Nofret.

'Devil and serpent! Evil one! Wait and see what we will do to you.'

With all the force of her arm she struck Nofret in the face. Renisenb gave a cry and caught her arm before she could repeat the blow.

'Kait—Kait—you must not do that.'

'Who says so? Let Nofret look to herself. She is only one here among many.'

Nofret stood quite still. The print of Kait's hand showed clear and red on her cheek. By the corner of the eye, where a bangle Kait wore on her wrist had cut the skin, a small trickle of blood was running down her face.

But it was Nofret's expression that puzzled Renisenb— yes, and frightened her. Nofret showed no anger. Instead there was a queer, exultant look in her eyes, and once more her mouth was curving up in its cat-like, satisfied smile.

'Thank you, Kait,' she said.

Then she walked on into the house.

*

Humming softly under her breath, her eyelids lowered, Nofret called Henet.

Henet came running, stopped, exclaimed. Nofret cut short her exclamations.

'Fetch me Kameni. Tell him to bring his pencase and ink and papyrus. There is a letter to be written to the master.'

Henet's eyes were fixed on Nofret's cheek.

'To the master . . . I see . . .'

Then she asked: 'Who did—that?'

'Kait.' Nofret smiled quietly and reminiscently.

Henet shook her head and clicked her tongue.

'All this is very bad—very bad . . . certainly the master must know of it.' She darted a quick, sideways look at Nofret. 'Yes, certainly Imhotep must know.'

Nofret said smoothly: 'You and I, Henet, think alike . . . I thought that we should do so.'

From the corner of her linen robe she detached a jewel of amethyst set in gold and placed it in the woman's hand.

'You and I, Henet, have Imhotep's true welfare at heart.'

'This is too good for me, Nofret . . . You are too generous . . . such a lovely bit of workmanship.'

'Imhotep and I appreciate fidelity.'

Nofret was still smiling, her eyes narrow and cat-like.

'Fetch Kameni,' she said. 'And come with him. You and he together are witnesses of what has occurred.'

Kameni came a little unwillingly, his brow puckered.

Nofret spoke imperiously:

'You remember Imhotep's instructions—before he left?'

'Yes,' said Kameni.

'The time has come,' said Nofret. 'Sit and take ink and

write as I tell you.' Then as Kameni still hesitated, she said impatiently, 'What you write shall be what you have seen with your own eyes and heard with your own ears—and Henet shall confirm all I say. The letter must be despatched with all secrecy and speed.'

Kameni said slowly, 'I do not like—'

Nofret flashed out at him: 'I have no complaint against Renisenb. Renisenb is soft, weak and a fool, but she has not tried to harm me. Does that content you?'

The colour of Kameni's bronze face deepened.

'I was not thinking of that—'

Nofret said smoothly:

'I think you were . . . Come now—fulfil your instructions—write.'

'Yes, write,' said Henet. 'I'm so distressed by all this—so terribly distressed. Certainly Imhotep must know about it. It's only right that he should. However unpleasant a thing is, one has to do one's duty. I've always felt that.'

Nofret laughed softly.

'I'm sure you have, Henet. You shall do your duty! And Kameni shall do his office. And I—I shall do what it is my pleasure to do . . .'

But still Kameni hesitated. His face was sullen—almost angry.

'I do not like this,' he said. 'Nofret, you had better take a little time to think.'

'*You* say that to *me*!'

Kameni flushed at her tone. His eyes avoided hers, but his sullen expression remained.

'Be careful, Kameni,' said Nofret smoothly. 'I have great

influence with Imhotep. He listens to what I say—so far he has been pleased with you—' She paused significantly.

'Are you threatening me, Nofret?' asked Kameni, angrily.

'Perhaps.'

He looked angrily at her for a moment or two—then he bent his head.

'I will do as you say, Nofret, but I think—yes, I think—that you will be sorry.'

'Are *you* threatening *me*, Kameni?'

'I am warning you . . .'

CHAPTER 8

Second Month of Winter 10th Day

Day followed day, and Renisenb sometimes felt that she was living in a dream.

She had made no more timid overtures to Nofret. She was, now, afraid of Nofret. There was something about Nofret she did not understand.

After the scene in the courtyard that day, Nofret had changed. There was a complacency about her, an exultation, that Renisenb could not fathom. Sometimes she thought that her own vision of Nofret as profoundly unhappy must have been ridiculously wrong. Nofret seemed pleased with life and herself and her surroundings.

And yet, actually, her surroundings had very definitely changed for the worse. In the days following Imhotep's departure, Nofret had quite deliberately, Renisenb thought, set out to sow dissension between the various members of Imhotep's family.

Now that family had closed its ranks solidly against the invader. There were no more dissensions between Satipy and Kait—no railing of Satipy against the unfortunate

Yahmose. Sobek seemed quieter and boasted less. Ipy was less impudent and offhand with his elder brothers. There seemed a new harmony between the family yet this harmony did not bring peace of mind to Renisenb—for with it went a curious, persistent undercurrent of illwill to Nofret.

The two women, Satipy and Kait, no longer quarrelled with her—they avoided her. They never spoke to her, and wherever she came they immediately gathered the children together and went elsewhere. At the same time, queer, annoying little accidents began to happen. A linen dress of Nofret's was spoilt with an over-hot iron—some dye stuff was spilt over another. Sometimes sharp thorns found their way into her clothing—a scorpion was discovered by her bed. The food that was served to her was over-seasoned— or lacking in any seasoning. There was a dead mouse one day in her portion of bread.

It was a quiet, relentless, petty persecution—nothing overt, nothing to lay hold of—it was essentially a woman's campaign.

Then, one day, old Esa sent for Satipy, Kait and Renisenb. Henet was already there, shaking her head and rubbing her hands in the background.

'Ha!' said Esa, peering at them with her usual ironical expression. 'So here are my clever granddaughters. What do you think you are doing, all of you? What is this I hear about Nofret's dress being ruined—and her food uneatable?'

Satipy and Kait both smiled. They were not nice smiles. Satipy said, 'Has Nofret complained?'

'No,' said Esa. She pushed the wig she always wore even in the house a little awry with one hand. 'No, Nofret has not complained. That is what worries me.'

'It does not worry *me*,' said Satipy, tossing her handsome head.

'Because you are a fool,' snapped Esa. 'Nofret has twice the brains of any of you three.'

'That remains to be seen,' said Satipy. She looked good-humoured and pleased with herself.

'What do you think you are all doing?' inquired Esa.

Satipy's face hardened.

'You are an old woman, Esa. I do not speak with any lack of respect—but things no longer matter to you in the way they matter to us who have husbands and young children. We have decided to take the matter into our own hands—we have ways of dealing with a woman whom we do not like and will not accept.'

'Fine words,' said Esa. 'Fine words.' She cackled. 'But a good discourse can be found with slave girls over the millstone.'

'A true and wise saying,' sighed Henet from the background.

Esa turned on her.

'Come, Henet, what does Nofret say to all this that is going on? You should know—you are always waiting on her.'

'As Imhotep told me to do. It is repugnant to me, of course—but I must do what the master ordered. You do not think I hope—'

Esa cut into the whining voice:

'We know all about you, Henet. Always devoted—and seldom thanked as you should be. What does Nofret say to all this? That is what I asked you.'

Henet shook her head.

'She says nothing. She just—smiles.'

'Exactly,' Esa picked up a jujube from a dish at her elbow, examined it and put it in her mouth. Then she said with sudden, malevolent acerbity:

'You are fools, all of you. The power is with Nofret, not with you. All you are doing is to play into her hands. I dare swear it even pleases her what you are doing.'

Satipy said sharply: 'Nonsense. Nofret is alone amongst many. What power has she?'

Esa said grimly:

'The power of a young, beautiful woman married to an ageing man. I know what I am talking about.' With a quick turn of her head she said: 'Henet knows what I am talking about!'

Henet started. She sighed and began to twist her hands.

'The master thinks a great deal of her—naturally—yes, quite naturally.'

'Go to the kitchen,' said Esa. 'Bring me some dates and some Syrian wine—yes, and honey too.'

When Henet had gone, the old woman said:

'There is mischief brewing—I can smell it. Satipy, you are the leader in all this. Be careful that while you are thinking yourself clever, you do not play into Nofret's hands.'

She leaned back and closed her eyes.

'I have warned you—now go.'

'We in Nofret's power, indeed!' said Satipy with a toss of her head as they went out to the lake. 'Esa is so old she gets the most extraordinary ideas into her head. It is we who have got Nofret in *our* power! We will do nothing against her that can be reported—but I think, yes, I think, that she will soon be sorry she ever came here.'

'You are cruel—cruel—' cried Renisenb.

Satipy looked amused.

'Do not pretend you love Nofret, Renisenb!'

'I do not. But you sound so—so *vindictive*.'

'I think of my children—and Yahmose! I am not a meek woman or one who brooks insult—and I have ambition. I would wring that woman's neck with the greatest of pleasure. Unfortunately it is not so simple as that. Imhotep's anger must not be roused. But I think—in the end—something may be managed.'

The letter came like a spearthrust to a fish.

Dumbfounded, silent, Yahmose, Sobek and Ipy stared at Hori as he read out the words from the papyrus scroll.

'Did I not tell Yahmose that I would hold him to blame if any harm came to my concubine? As you all live, I am against you and you are against me! I will no longer live with you in one house since you have not respected my concubine Nofret! You are no longer my son of my flesh. Neither are Sobek and Ipy my sons of my flesh. Each one of you has done harm to my concubine. That is

attested by Kameni and Henet. I will turn you out of my
house—each of you! I have supported you—now I will
no longer support you.'

Hori paused and went on:

'The ka servant Imhotep addresses Hori. To you who have
been faithful, how are you in your life, safety and health?
Salute my mother Esa for me and my daughter Renisenb
and greet Henet. Look after my affairs carefully until I
reach you and see that there be prepared for me a deed
whereby my concubine Nofret shall share with me in all
my property as my wife. Neither Yahmose, nor Sobek
shall be associated with me, nor will I support them, and
hereby I denounce them that they have done harm to my
concubine! Keep all safe till I come. How evil is it when a
man's household do evil deeds to his concubine. As for
Ipy, let him take warning, and if he does a single hurt to
my concubine, he too shall depart from my house.'

There was a paralysed silence, then Sobek rose up in a
violent rage.

'How has this come about? What has my father heard?
Who has been bearing false tales to him? Shall we endure
this? My father cannot disinherit us so and give all his
goods to his concubine!'

Hori said mildly:

'It will cause unfavourable comment—and it will not be
accepted as a right action—but legally it is in his power.
He can make a deed of settlement in any way he wishes.'

'She has bewitched him—that black, jeering serpent has put a spell upon him!'

Yahmose murmured as though dumbfounded:

'It is unbelievable—it cannot be true.'

'My father is mad—mad!' cried Ipy. 'He turns even against *me* at this woman's bidding!'

Hori said gravely:

'Imhotep will return shortly—that he says. By then his anger may have abated; he may not really mean to do as he says.'

There was a short, unpleasant laugh. It was Satipy who had laughed. She stood looking at them from the doorway into the women's quarters.

'So that is what we are to do, is it, most excellent Hori? Wait and see!'

Yahmose said slowly:

'What else can we do?'

'What else?' Satipy's voice rose. She screamed out:

'What have you got in your veins, all of you? Milk? Yahmose, I know, is not a man! But you, Sobek—have you no remedy for these ills? A knife in the heart and the girl could do us no more harm.'

'Satipy,' cried Yahmose. 'My father would never forgive us!'

'So you say. But I tell you a dead concubine is not the same as a live concubine! Once she was dead, his heart would return to his sons and their children. And besides, how should he know *how* she died? We could say a scorpion stung her! We are together in this, are we not?'

Yahmose said slowly:

'My father *would* know. Henet would tell him.'

Satipy gave a hysterical laugh.

'Most prudent Yahmose! Most gentle, cautious Yahmose! It is *you* who should look after the children and do woman's work in the back of the house. Sakhmet help me! Married to a man who is not a man. And *you*, Sobek, for all your bluster, what courage have you, what determination? I swear by Ra, I am a better man than either of you.'

She swung round and went out.

Kait, who had been standing behind her, came a step forward.

She said, her voice deep and shaken:

'It is true what Satipy says! She is a better man than any of you. Yahmose, Sobek, Ipy—will you all sit here doing nothing? What of our children, Sobek? Cast out to starve! Very well, if *you* will do nothing, *I* will. You are none of you *men*!'

As she in turn went out, Sobek sprang to his feet.

'By the Nine Gods of the Ennead, Kait is right! There is a man's work to be done—and we sit here talking and shaking our heads.'

He strode towards the door. Hori called after him:

'Sobek, Sobek, where are you going? What are you going to do?'

Sobek, handsome and fierce, shouted from the doorway:

'I shall do *something*—that is clear. And what I do I shall *enjoy* doing!'

CHAPTER 9

Second Month of Winter 10th Day

Renisenb came out on to the porch and stood there for a moment, shielding her eyes against the sudden glare.

She felt sick and shaken and full of a nameless fear. She said to herself, repeating the words over and over again mechanically:

'I must warn Nofret . . . I must warn her . . .'

Behind her, in the house, she could hear men's voices, those of Hori and Yahmose blending into each other, and above them, shrill and clear, the boyish tones of Ipy.

'Satipy and Kait are right. There are no men in this family! But *I* am a man. Yes, I am a man in heart if not in years. Nofret has jeered at me, laughed at me; treated me as a child. I will show her that I am *not* a child. I am not afraid of my father's anger. I know my father. He is bewitched—the woman has put a spell on him. If she were destroyed his heart would come back to me—to *me*! I am the son he loves best. You all treat me as a child—but you shall see. Yes, you shall see!'

Rushing out of the house he collided with Renisenb and

almost knocked her down. She clutched at his sleeve.

'Ipy, Ipy, where are you going?'

'To find Nofret. She shall see whether she can laugh at me!'

'Wait a little. You must calm down. We must none of us do anything rash.'

'Rash?' The boy laughed scornfully. 'You are like Yahmose. Prudence! Caution! Nothing must be done in a hurry! Yahmose is an old woman. And Sobek is all words and boasting. Let go of me, Renisenb.'

He twitched the linen of his sleeve from her grasp.

'Nofret, where *is* Nofret?'

Henet, who had just come bustling out from the house, murmured:

'Oh dear, this is a bad business—a very bad business. What will become of us all? What would my dear mistress say?'

'Where is Nofret, Henet?'

Renisenb cried: 'Don't tell him,' but Henet was already answering:

'She went out the back way. Down towards the flax fields.'

Ipy rushed back through the house and Renisenb said reproachfully: 'You should not have told him, Henet.'

'You don't trust old Henet. You never have confidence in me.' The whine in her voice became more pronounced. 'But poor old Henet knows what she is doing. The boy needs time to cool off. He won't find Nofret by the flax fields.' She grinned. 'Nofret is here—in the pavilion—with Kameni.'

She nodded her head across the courtyard.

And she added with what seemed rather disproportionate stress:

'With Kameni . . .'

But Renisenb had already started to cross the courtyard.

Teti, dragging her wooden lion, came running from the lake to her mother and Renisenb caught her up in her arms. She knew, as she held the child to her, the force that was driving Satipy and Kait. These women were fighting for their children.

Teti gave a little fretful cry.

'Not so tight, mother, not so tight. You are hurting me.'

Renisenb put the child down. She went slowly across the courtyard. On the far side of the pavilion Nofret and Kameni were standing together. They turned as Renisenb approached.

Renisenb spoke quickly and breathlessly.

'Nofret, I have come to warn you. You must be careful. You must guard yourself.'

A look of contemptuous amusement passed over Nofret's face.

'So the dogs are howling?'

'They are very angry—they will do some harm to you.'

Nofret shook her head.

'No one can harm me,' she said, with a superb confidence. 'If they did, it would be reported to your father—and he would exact vengeance. They will know that when they pause to think.' She laughed. 'What fools they have been— with their petty insults and persecutions! It was *my* game they played all the time.'

Renisenb said slowly:

'So you have planned for this all along? And I was sorry
for you—I thought we were unkind! I am not sorry any
longer . . . I think, Nofret, that you are *wicked*. When you
come to deny the forty-two sins at the hour of judgement
you will not be able to say "I have done no evil." Nor will
you be able to say "I have not been covetous." And your
heart that is being weighed in the scales against the feather
of truth will sink in the balance.'

Nofret said sullenly:

'You are very pious all of a sudden. But I have not
harmed *you*, Renisenb. I said nothing against you. Ask
Kameni if that is not so.'

Then she walked across the courtyard and up the steps
to the porch. Henet came out to meet her and the two
women went into the house.

Renisenb turned slowly to Kameni.

'So it was *you*, Kameni, who helped her to do this
to us?'

Kameni said eagerly:

'Are you angry with me, Renisenb? But what could I
do? Before Imhotep left he charged me solemnly that I was
to write at Nofret's bidding at any time she might ask me
to do so. Say you do not blame me, Renisenb. What else
could I do?'

'I cannot blame you,' said Renisenb slowly. 'You had, I
suppose, to carry out my father's orders.'

'I did not like doing it—and it is true, Renisenb, there
was not one word said against *you*.'

'As if I cared about that!'

'But I do. Whatever Nofret had told me, I would not have written one word that might harm *you*, Renisenb—please believe me.'

Renisenb shook her head perplexedly. The point Kameni was labouring to make seemed of little importance to her. She felt hurt and angry as though Kameni, in some way, had failed her. Yet he was, after all, a stranger. Though allied by blood, he was nevertheless a stranger whom her father had brought from a distant part of the country. He was a junior scribe who had been given a task by his employer, and who had obediently carried it out.

'I wrote no more than truth,' Kameni persisted. 'There were no lies set down, that I swear to you.'

'No,' said Renisenb. 'There would be no lies. Nofret is too clever for that.'

Old Esa had, after all, been right. That persecution over which Satipy and Kait had gloated had been just exactly what Nofret had wanted. No wonder that she had gone about smiling her cat-like smile.

'She is bad,' said Renisenb, following out her thoughts. 'Yes!'

Kameni assented. 'Yes,' he said. 'She is an evil creature.'

Renisenb turned and looked at him curiously.

'You knew her before she came here, did you not? You knew her in Memphis?'

Kameni flushed and looked uncomfortable.

'I did not know her well . . . I had heard of her. A proud girl, they said, ambitious and hard—and one who did not forgive.'

Renisenb flung back her head in sudden impatience.

'I do not believe it,' she said. 'My father will not do what he threatens. He is angry at present—but he could not be so unjust. When he comes he will forgive.'

'When he comes,' said Kameni, 'Nofret will see to it that he does not change his mind. You do not know Nofret, Renisenb. She is very clever and determined—and she is, remember, very beautiful.'

'Yes,' admitted Renisenb. 'She is beautiful.'

She got up. For some reason the thought of Nofret's beauty hurt her . . .

Renisenb spent the afternoon playing with the children. As she took part in their game, the vague ache in her heart lessened. It was not until just before sunset that she stood upright, smoothing back her hair and the pleats of her dress which had got crumpled and disarranged, and wondered vaguely why neither Satipy nor Kait had been out as usual.

Kameni had long gone from the courtyard. Renisenb went slowly across into the house. There was no one in the living-room and she passed through to the back of the house and the women's quarters. Esa was nodding in the corner of her room and her little slave girl was marking piles of linen sheets. They were baking batches of triangular loaves in the kitchen. There was no one else about.

A curious emptiness pressed on Renisenb's spirits. Where was everyone?

Hori had probably gone up to the Tomb. Yahmose might be with him or out on the fields. Sobek and Ipy would be with the cattle or possibly seeing to the cornbins.

But where were Satipy and Kait, and where, yes, where was Nofret?

The strong perfume of Nofret's unguent filled her empty room. Renisenb stood in the doorway staring at the little wood pillow, at a jewel box, at a heap of bead bracelets and a ring set with a blue glazed scarab. Perfumes, unguents, clothes, linens, sandals—all speaking of their owner, of Nofret who lived in their midst and who was a stranger and an enemy.

Where, Renisenb wondered, could Nofret herself be?

She went slowly towards the back entrance of the house and met Henet coming in.

'Where is everybody, Henet? The house is empty except for my grandmother.'

'How should *I* know, Renisenb? I have been working—helping with the weaving, seeing to a thousand and one things. *I* have no time for going for walks.'

That meant, thought Renisenb, that somebody had gone for a walk. Perhaps Satipy had followed Yahmose up to the Tomb to harangue further? But where was Kait? Unlike Kait to be away from her children for so long.

And again, a strange disturbing undercurrent, there ran the thought:

'Where is Nofret?'

As though Henet had read the thought in her mind, she supplied the answer.

'As for Nofret, she went off a long time ago up to the Tomb. Oh well, Hori is a match for her.' Henet laughed spitefully. 'Hori has brains too.' She sidled a little closer to Renisenb. 'I wish you knew, Renisenb, how unhappy I've been over all this. She came to me, you know, that day—with the mark of Kait's fingers on her cheek and the blood streaming down. And she got Kameni to write and me to say what I'd seen—and of course I couldn't say I *hadn't* seen it! Oh, she's a clever one. And I, thinking all the time of your dear mother—'

Renisenb pushed past her and went out into the golden glow of the evening sun. Deep shadows were on the cliffs—the whole world looked fantastic at this hour of sunset.

Renisenb's steps quickened as she took the way to the cliff path. She would go up to the Tomb—find Hori. Yes, find Hori. It was what she had done as a child when her toys had been broken—when she had been uncertain or afraid. Hori was like the cliffs themselves, steadfast, immovable, unchanging.

Renisenb thought confusedly: Everything will be all right when I get to Hori . . .

Her steps quickened—she was almost running.

Then suddenly she saw Satipy coming towards her. Satipy, too, must have been up to the Tomb.

What a very odd way Satipy was walking, swaying from side to side, stumbling as though she could not see . . .

When Satipy saw Renisenb she stopped short, her hand went to her breast. Renisenb, drawing close, was startled at the sight of Satipy's face.

'What's the matter, Satipy, are you ill?'

Satipy's voice in answer was a croak, her eyes were shifting from side to side.

'No, no, of course not.'

'You look ill. You look frightened. What has happened?'

93

'What should have happened? Nothing, of course.'

'Where have you been?'

'I went up to the Tomb—to find Yahmose. He was not there. No one was there.'

Renisenb still stared. This was a new Satipy—a Satipy with all the spirit and resolution drained out of her.

'Come, Renisenb—come back to the house.'

Satipy put a slightly shaking hand on Renisenb's arm, urging her back the way she had come and at the touch Renisenb felt a sudden revolt.

'No, I am going up to the Tomb.'

'There is no one there, I tell you.'

'I like to look over the river. To sit there.'

'But the sun is setting—it is too late.'

Satipy's fingers closed vice-like over Renisenb's arm. Renisenb wrenched herself loose.

'Let me go, Satipy.'

'No. Come back. Come back with me.'

But Renisenb had already broken loose, pushed past her, and was on her way to the cliff.

There was something—instinct told her there was *something* . . . Her steps quickened to a run . . .

Then she saw it—the dark bundle lying under the shadow of the cliff . . . She hurried along until she stood close beside it.

There was no surprise in her at what she saw. It was as though already she had expected it . . .

Nofret lay with her face upturned, her body broken and twisted. Her eyes were open and sightless . . .

Renisenb bent and touched the cold stiff cheek then stood

up again looking down at her. She hardly heard Satipy come up behind her.

'She must have fallen,' Satipy was saying. 'She has fallen. She was walking along the cliff path and she fell . . .'

Yes, Renisenb thought, that was what had happened. Nofret had fallen from the path above, her body bouncing off the limestone rocks.

'She may have seen a snake,' said Satipy, 'and been startled. There are snakes asleep in the sun on that path sometimes.'

Snakes. Yes, snakes. *Sobek and the snake*. A snake, its back broken, lying dead in the sun. Sobek, his eyes gleaming . . .

She thought: *Sobek . . . Nofret . . .*

Then sudden relief came to her as she heard Hori's voice. 'What has happened?'

She turned with relief. Hori and Yahmose had come up together. Satipy was explaining eagerly that Nofret must have fallen from the path above.

Yahmose said, 'She must have come up to find us, but Hori and I have been out to look at the irrigation canals. We have been away at least an hour. As we came back we saw you standing here.'

Renisenb said, and her voice surprised her, it sounded so different: '*Where is Sobek?*'

She felt rather than saw Hori's immediate sharp turn of the head at the question. Yahmose sounded merely puzzled as he said:

'Sobek? I have not seen him all the afternoon. Not since he left us so angrily in the house.'

But Hori was looking at Renisenb. She raised her eyes

and met his. She saw him turn from their gaze and look down thoughtfully at Nofret's body and she knew with absolute certainty exactly what he was thinking.

He murmured questioningly:

'Sobek?'

'Oh no,' Renisenb heard herself saying. 'Oh no . . . Oh *no* . . .'

Satipy said again urgently: '*She fell from the path.* It is narrow just above here—and dangerous . . .'

Sobek liked killing. '*What I do, I shall enjoy doing* . . .'

Sobek killing a snake . . .

Sobek meeting Nofret on that narrow path . . .

She heard herself murmuring brokenly:

'We don't know—we don't *know* . . .'

And then, with intimate relief, with the sense of a burden taken away, she heard Hori's grave voice giving weight and value to Satipy's asseveration.

'She must have fallen from the path . . .'

His eyes met Renisenb's. She thought: 'He and I know . . . We shall always know . . .'

Aloud she heard her voice saying shakily:

'She fell from the path . . .'

And like a final echo, Yahmose's gentle voice chimed in.

'She must have fallen from the path.'

CHAPTER 10

Fourth Month of Winter 6th Day

Imhotep sat facing Esa.

'They all tell the same story,' he said fretfully.

'That is at least convenient,' said Esa.

'Convenient—convenient? What extraordinary words you use!'

Esa gave a short cackle.

'I know what I am saying, my son.'

'Are they speaking the truth, that is what *I* have to decide!' Imhotep spoke portentously.

'You are hardly the goddess Maat. Nor, like Anubis, can you weigh the heart in a balance!'

'Was it an accident?' Imhotep shook his head judicially. 'I have to remember that the announcement of my intentions towards my ungrateful family may have aroused some passionate feelings.'

'Yes, indeed,' said Esa. 'Feelings were aroused. They shouted so in the main hall that I could hear what was said in my room here. By the way, were those *really* your intentions?'

Imhotep shifted uneasily as he murmured:

'I wrote in anger—in justifiable anger. My family needed teaching a sharp lesson.'

'In other words,' said Esa, 'you were merely giving them a fright. Is that it?'

'My dear mother, does that matter now?'

'I see,' said Esa. 'You did not know what you meant to do. Muddled thinking as usual.'

Imhotep controlled his irritation with an effort.

'I simply mean that that particular point no longer arises. It is the facts of Nofret's death that are now in question. If I were to believe that anyone in my family could be so undutiful, so unbalanced in their anger, as wantonly to harm the girl—I—I really do not know what I should do!'

'So it is fortunate,' said Esa, 'that they all tell the same story! Nobody has hinted at anything else, have they?'

'Certainly not.'

'Then why not regard the incident as closed? You should have taken the girl North with you. I told you so at the time.'

'Then you *do* believe—'

Esa said with emphasis:

'I believe what I am told, unless it conflicts with what I have seen with my own eyes (which is very little nowadays), or heard with my own ears. You have questioned Henet, I suppose? What has she to say of the matter?'

'She is deeply distressed—very distressed. On my behalf.'

Esa raised her eyebrows.

'Indeed. You surprise me.'

'Henet,' said Imhotep warmly, 'has a lot of heart.'

'Quite so. She has also more than the usual allowance of tongue. If distress at your loss is her only reaction, I should certainly regard the incident as closed. There are plenty of other affairs to occupy your attention.'

'Yes, indeed.' Imhotep rose with a reassumption of his fussy, important manner. 'Yahmose is waiting for me now in the main hall with all sorts of matters needing my urgent attention. There are many decisions awaiting my sanction. As you say, private grief must not usurp the main functions of life.'

He hurried out.

Esa smiled for a moment, a somewhat sardonic smile, then her face grew grave again. She sighed and shook her head.

Yahmose was awaiting his father with Kameni in attendance. Hori, Yahmose explained, was superintending the work of the embalmers and undertakers who were busy with the last stages of the funeral preparations.

It had taken Imhotep some weeks to journey home after receiving the news of Nofret's death, and the funeral preparations were now almost completed. The body had received its long soaking in the brine bath, had been restored to some semblance of its normal appearance, had been oiled and rubbed with salts, and duly wrapped in its bandages and deposited in its coffin.

Yahmose explained that he had appointed a small funeral chamber near the rock tomb designed later to hold the body of Imhotep himself. He went into the details of what he had ordered and Imhotep expressed his approval.

'You have done well, Yahmose,' he said kindly. 'You seem to have shown very good judgement and to have kept your head well.'

Yahmose coloured a little at this unexpected praise.

'Ipi and Montu are, of course, expensive embalmers,' went on Imhotep. 'These canopic jars, for instance, seem to me unduly costly. There is really no need for such extravagance. Some of their charges seem to me much too high. That is the worst of these embalmers who have been employed by the Governor's family. They think they can charge any fantastic prices they like. It would have come much cheaper to go to somebody less well known.'

'In your absence,' said Yahmose, 'I had to decide on these matters—and I was anxious that all honour should be paid to a concubine for whom you had so great a regard.'

Imhotep nodded and patted Yahmose's shoulder.

'It was a fault on the right side, my son. You are, I know, usually most prudent in money matters. I appreciate that in this matter, any unnecessary expense was incurred in order to please me. All the same, I am not made of money, and a concubine is—er ahem!—only a concubine. We will cancel, I think, the more expensive of the amulets—and let me see, there are one or two other ways of cutting down the fees . . . Just read out the items of the estimate, Kameni.'

Kameni rustled the papyrus.

Yahmose breathed a sigh of relief.

Kait, coming slowly out from the house to the lake, paused where the children and their mothers were.

'You were right, Satipy,' she said. 'A dead concubine is *not* the same as a live concubine!'

Satipy looked up at her, her eyes vague and unseeing. It was Renisenb who asked quickly:

'What do you mean, Kait?'

'For a live concubine, nothing was too good—clothes, jewels—even the inheritance of Imhotep's own flesh and blood! But now Imhotep is busy cutting down the cost of the funeral expenses! After all, why waste money on a dead woman? Yes, Satipy, you were right.'

Satipy murmured: 'What did I say? I have forgotten.'

'It is best so,' agreed Kait. 'I, too, have forgotten. And Renisenb also.'

Renisenb looked at Kait without speaking. There had been something in Kait's voice—something faintly menacing, that impressed Renisenb disagreeably. She had always been accustomed to think of Kait as rather a stupid woman—someone gentle and submissive, but rather negligible. It struck her now that Kait and Satipy seemed to have changed places. Satipy the dominant and aggressive was subdued—almost timid. It was the quiet Kait who now seemed to domineer over Satipy.

But people, thought Renisenb, do not really change their characters—or do they? She felt confused. Had Kait and Satipy *really* changed in the last few weeks, or was the change in the one the result of the change in the other? Was it Kait who had grown aggressive? Or did she merely *seem* so because of the sudden collapse of Satipy?

Satipy definitely *was* different. Her voice was no longer upraised in the familiar shrewish accents. She crept round the courtyard and the house with a nervous, shrinking gait quite unlike her usual self-assured manner. Renisenb had put down the change in her to the shock of Nofret's death, but it was incredible that that shock could last so long. It would have been far more like Satipy, Renisenb could not but think, to have exulted openly in a matter of fact manner over the concubine's sudden and untimely death. As it was, she shrank nervously whenever Nofret's name was mentioned. Even Yahmose seemed to be exempt from her hectoring and bullying and had, in consequence, begun to assume a more resolute demeanour himself. At any rate, the change in Satipy was all to the good—or at least so Renisenb supposed. Yet something about it made her vaguely uneasy . . .

Suddenly, with a start, Renisenb became aware that Kait was looking at her, was frowning. Kait, she realized, was waiting for a word of assent to something she had just said.

'Renisenb also,' repeated Kait, 'has forgotten.'

Suddenly Renisenb felt a flood of revolt overwhelm her. Neither Kait, nor Satipy, nor anyone should dictate to her what she should or should not remember. She returned Kait's look steadily with a distinct hint of defiance.

'The women of a household,' said Kait, 'must stand together.'

Renisenb found her voice. She said clearly and defiantly: 'Why?'

'Because their interests are the same.'

Renisenb shook her head violently. She thought, confusedly, 'I am a person as well as a woman. I am Renisenb.'

Aloud she said: 'It is not so simple as that.'

'Do you want to make trouble, Renisenb?'

'No. And anyway, what do you mean by trouble?'

'Everything that was said that day in the big hall had best be forgotten.'

Renisenb laughed.

'You are stupid, Kait. The servants, the slaves, my grandmother—everyone must have overheard! Why pretend that things did not happen that did happen?'

'We were angry,' said Satipy in a dull voice. 'We did not mean what we said.'

She added with a feverish irritability:

'Stop talking about it, Kait. If Renisenb wants to make trouble, let her.'

'I don't want to make trouble,' said Renisenb, indignantly. 'But it is stupid to *pretend*.'

'No,' said Kait. 'It is wisdom. You have Teti to consider.'

'Teti is all right.'

'Everything is all right—*now that Nofret is dead*,' Kait smiled.

It was a serene, quiet, satisfied smile—and again Renisenb felt a tide of revolt rise in her.

Yet what Kait said was true. Now that Nofret was dead everything was all right.

Satipy, Kait, herself, the children . . . All secure—all at peace—with no apprehensions for the future. The intruder, the disturbing, menacing stranger, had departed—for ever.

Then why this stirring of an emotion that she did not understand on Nofret's behalf? Why this feeling of

103

championship for the dead girl whom she had not liked? Nofret was wicked and Nofret was dead—could she not leave it at that? Why this sudden stab of pity—of something more than pity—something that was almost comprehension?

Renisenb shook her head perplexedly. She sat on there by the water after the others had gone in, trying vainly to understand the confusion in her mind.

The sun was low when Hori, crossing the courtyard, saw her and came to sit beside her.

'It is late, Renisenb. The sun is setting. You should go in.' His grave, quiet voice soothed her, as always. She turned to him with a question.

'*Must* the women of a household stick together?'

'Who has been saying that to you, Renisenb?'

'Kait. She and Satipy—'

Renisenb broke off.

'And you—want to think for yourself?'

'Oh, *think*! I do not know how to think, Hori. Everything is confused in my head. *People* are confused. Everybody is different from what I thought they were. Satipy I always thought was bold, resolute, domineering. But now she is weak, vacillating, even timid. Then which is the real Satipy? People cannot change like that in a day.'

'Not in a day—no.'

'And Kait—she who was always meek and submissive and let everybody bully her. Now she dominates us all! Even Sobek seems afraid of her. And even Yahmose is different—he gives orders and expects them to be obeyed!'

'And all this confuses you, Renisenb?'

'Yes. Because I do not *understand*. I feel sometimes that even Henet may be quite different from what she appears to be!'

Renisenb laughed as though at an absurdity, but Hori did not join her. His face remained grave and thoughtful.

'You have never thought very much about people, have you, Renisenb? If you had you would realize—' He paused and then went on. 'You know that in all tombs there is always a false door?'

Renisenb stared. 'Yes, of course.'

'Well, people are like that too. They create a false door—to deceive. If they are conscious of weakness, of inefficiency, they make an imposing door of self-assertion, of bluster, of overwhelming authority—and, after a time, they get to believe in it themselves. They think, and everybody thinks, that they *are* like that. But behind that door, Renisenb, is bare rock . . . And so when reality comes and touches them with the feather of truth—their true self reasserts itself. For Kait gentleness and submission brought her all she desired—a husband and children. Stupidity made life easier for her—but when reality in the form of danger threatened, her true nature appeared. She did not change, Renisenb—that strength and that ruthlessness were always there.'

Renisenb said childishly: 'But I do not like it, Hori. It makes me afraid. Everyone being different from what I thought them. And what about myself? *I* am always the same.'

'Are you?' He smiled at her. 'Then why have you sat here all these hours, your forehead puckered, brooding and

105

thinking? Did the old Renisenb—the Renisenb who went away with Khay—ever do that?'

'Oh no. There was no need—' Renisenb stopped.

'You see? You have said it yourself. That is the word of reality—*need*! You are not the happy, unthinking child you have always appeared to be, accepting everything at its face value. You are not just one of the women of the household. You are Renisenb who wants to think for herself, who wonders about other people . . .'

Renisenb said slowly: 'I have been wondering about Nofret . . .'

'What have you been wondering?'

'I have been wondering why I cannot forget her . . . She was bad and cruel and tried to do us harm and she is dead—why can I not leave it at that?'

'Can you not leave it at that?'

'No. I try to—but—' Renisenb paused. She passed her hand across her eyes perplexedly. 'Sometimes I feel I *know* about Nofret, Hori.'

'Know? What do you mean?'

'I can't explain. But it comes to me every now and then—almost as though she were here, beside me. I feel—almost—as though I were her—I seem to know what she felt. She was very unhappy, Hori, I know that now, though I didn't at the time. She wanted to hurt us all *because* she was so unhappy.'

'You cannot know that, Renisenb.'

'No, of course I cannot *know* it, but it is what I *feel*. That misery, that bitterness, that black hate—I saw it in her face once, and I did not understand! She must have loved someone and then something went wrong—perhaps he died . . . or went away—but it left her like that—wanting to hurt—to wound. Oh! you may say what you like, I know I am right! She became a concubine to that old man, my father—and she came here, and we disliked her—and she thought she would make us all as unhappy as she was—Yes, that was how it was!'

Hori looked at her curiously.

'How sure you sound, Renisenb. And yet you did not know Nofret well.'

'But I feel it is *true*, Hori. I feel *her*—Nofret. Sometimes I feel her quite close beside me . . .'

'I see.'

There was a silence between them. It was almost dark now.

Then Hori said quietly: 'You believe, do you not, that Nofret did not die by accident? You think she was thrown down?'

Renisenb felt a passionate repugnance at hearing her belief put into words.

'No, no, don't say it.'

'But I think, Renisenb, we had better say it—since it is in your head. You *do* think so?'

'I—yes!'

Hori bent his head thoughtfully. He went on:

'And you think it was Sobek who did it?'

'Who else could it have been? You remember him with the snake? And you remember what he said—that day—the day of her death—before he went out of the great hall?'

'I remember what he said, yes. But it is not always the people who *say* most who *do* most!'

107

'But don't you believe she *was* killed?'

'Yes, Renisenb, I do ... But it is, after all, only an opinion. I have no proof. I do not think there ever can be proof. That is why I have encouraged Imhotep to accept the verdict of accident. Someone pushed Nofret—we shall never know who it was.'

'You mean, you don't think it *was* Sobek?'

'*I* do not think so. But as I say, we can never know—so it is best not to think about it.'

'But—if it was not Sobek—who do you think it was?'

Hori shook his head.

'If I have an idea—it may be the wrong idea. So it is better not to say . . .'

'But then—we shall never know!'

There was dismay in Renisenb's voice.

'Perhaps—' Hori hesitated—'perhaps that may be the best thing.'

'Not to know?'

'Not to know.'

Renisenb shivered.

'But then—oh, Hori, I am afraid!'

PART THREE

Summer

CHAPTER 11

First Month of Summer 11th Day

The final ceremonies had been completed and the incantations duly spoken. Montu, a Divine Father of the Temple of Hathor, took the broom of *heden* grass and carefully swept out the chamber whilst he recited the charm to remove the footprints of all evil spirits before the door was sealed up for ever.

Then the Tomb was sealed, and all that remained of the embalmers' work, pots full of natron, salt and rags that had been in contact with the body, were placed in a little chamber nearby, and that too was sealed.

Imhotep squared his shoulders and took a deep breath, relaxing his devout funeral expression. Everything had been done in a befitting manner. Nofret had been buried with all the prescribed rites and with no sparing of expense (somewhat undue expense in Imhotep's opinion).

Imhotep exchanged courtesies with the Priests who, their sacred office now finished, reassumed their men of the world manner. Everyone descended to the house where suitable refreshments were waiting. Imhotep discussed with the principal Divine Father the recent political changes. Thebes was rapidly becoming a very powerful city. It was possible that Egypt might once more be united under one ruler before very long. The Golden Age of the Pyramid builders might return.

Montu spoke with reverence and approval of the King Nebhepet-Re. A first-class soldier and a man of piety also. The corrupt and cowardly North could hardly stand against him. A unified Egypt, that was what was needed. And it would mean, undoubtedly, great things for Thebes . . .

The men walked together, discussing the future.

Renisenb looked back at the cliff and the sealed tomb chamber.

'So that is the end,' she murmured. A feeling of relief swept over her. She had feared she hardly knew what! Some last minute outburst or accusation? But everything had gone with commendable smoothness. Nofret was duly buried with all the rites of religion.

It was the end.

Henet said below her breath: 'I hope so, I'm sure I hope so, Renisenb.'

Renisenb turned on her.

'What do you mean, Henet?'

Henet avoided her eyes.

'I just said I hoped that it *was* the end. Sometimes what you think is an end is only a beginning. And that wouldn't do at all.'

Renisenb said angrily: 'What are you talking about, Henet? What are you hinting at?'

'I'm sure I never hint, Renisenb. I wouldn't do such a

thing. Nofret's buried and everyone's satisfied. So everything is as it should be.'

Renisenb demanded: 'Did my father ask you what *you* thought about Nofret's death?'

'Yes, indeed, Renisenb. Most particular, he was, that I should tell him exactly what I thought about it all.'

'And what did you tell him?'

'Well, of course I said it was an accident. What else could it have been? You don't think for a minute, I said, that anyone in your family would harm the girl, do you? They wouldn't dare, I said. They've far too much respect for you. Grumble they might, but nothing more, I said. You can take it from me, I said, that there's been nothing of *that* kind!'

Henet nodded her head and chuckled.

'And my father believed you?'

Again Henet nodded with a good deal of satisfaction.

'Ah, your father knows how devoted I am to his interests. He'll always take old Henet's word for anything. *He* appreciates me if none of the rest of you do. Ah well, my devotion to all of you is its own reward. I don't expect thanks.'

'You were devoted to Nofret, too,' said Renisenb.

'I'm sure I don't know what gave you that idea, Renisenb. I had to obey orders like everyone else.'

'She thought you were devoted to her.'

Henet chuckled again.

'Nofret wasn't quite as clever as she thought herself. A proud girl—and a girl who thought she owned the earth. Well, she's got the judges in the underworld to satisfy now—and a pretty face won't help her there. At any rate we're quit of her. At least,' she added under her breath and touching one of the amulets she wore, 'I hope so.'

'Renisenb, I want to talk to you about Satipy.'

'Yes, Yahmose?'

Renisenb looked up sympathetically into her brother's gentle, worried face.

Yahmose said slowly and heavily: 'There is something very wrong the matter with Satipy. I cannot understand it.'

Renisenb shook her head sadly. She was at a loss to find anything comforting to say.

'I have noticed this change in her for some time,' went on Yahmose. 'She starts and trembles at any unaccustomed noise. She does not eat well. She creeps about as though—as though she were afraid of her own shadow. You must have noticed it, Renisenb?'

'Yes, indeed, we have all noticed it.'

'I have asked her if she is ill—if I should send for a physician—but she says there is nothing—that she is perfectly well.'

'I know.'

'So you have asked her that too? And she has said nothing to you—nothing at all?'

He laid stress on the words. Renisenb sympathized with his anxiety, but she could say nothing to help.

'She insists that she is quite well.'

Yahmose murmured. 'She does not sleep well at night—she cries out in her sleep. Is she—could she have some sorrow that we know nothing about?'

Renisenb shook her head.

'I do not see how that is possible. There is nothing wrong with the children. Nothing has happened here—except, of course, Nofret's death—and Satipy would hardly grieve for that,' she added dryly.

Yahmose smiled faintly.

'No, indeed. Quite the contrary. Besides, this has been coming on for some time. It began, I think, before Nofret's death.'

His tone was a little uncertain and Renisenb looked at him quickly. Yahmose said with mild persistence:

'*Before* Nofret's death, don't you think so?'

'I did not notice it until afterwards,' said Renisenb, slowly.

'And she has said nothing to you—you are sure?'

Renisenb shook her head. 'But you know, Yahmose, I do not think Satipy is ill. It seems to me more that she is—afraid.'

'Afraid?' exclaimed Yahmose, in great astonishment. 'But why should Satipy be afraid? And of what? Satipy has always had the courage of a lion.'

'I know,' said Renisenb, helplessly. 'We have always thought so—but people change—it is queer.'

'Does Kait know anything—do you think? Has Satipy spoken to her?'

'She would be more likely to talk to her than to me—but I do not think so. In fact, I am sure of it.'

'What does Kait think?'

'Kait? Kait never thinks about anything.'

All Kait had done, Renisenb was reflecting, was to take

advantage of Satipy's unusual meekness by grabbing for herself and her children the finest of the newly woven linen—a thing she would never have been allowed to do had Satipy been her usual self. The house would have resounded with passionate disputings! The fact that Satipy had given it up with hardly a murmur had impressed Renisenb more than anything else that could have happened.

'Have you spoken to Esa?' Renisenb asked. 'Our grand-mother is wise about women and their ways.'

'Esa,' said Yahmose with some slight annoyance, 'merely bids me be thankful for the change. She says it is too much to hope that Satipy will continue to be so sweetly reasonable.'

Renisenb said with some slight hesitation, 'Have you asked Henet?'

'Henet?' Yahmose frowned. 'No, indeed. I would not speak of such things to Henet. She takes far too much upon herself as it is. My father spoils her.'

'Oh, I know that. She is very tiresome. But all the same—well—' Renisenb hesitated—'Henet usually knows things.'

Yahmose said slowly: 'Would you ask her, Renisenb? And tell me what she says?'

'If you like.'

Renisenb put her query at a moment when she had Henet to herself. They were on their way to the weaving sheds. Rather to her surprise the question seemed to make Henet uneasy. There was none of her usual avidity to gossip.

She touched an amulet she was wearing and glanced over her shoulder.

'It's nothing to do with me, I'm sure . . . It's not for me to notice whether any one's themselves or not. I mind my own business. If there's trouble I don't want to be mixed up in it.'

'Trouble? What kind of trouble?'

Henet gave her a quick, sideways glance.

'None, I hope. None that need concern us, anyway. You and I, Renisenb, we've nothing to reproach ourselves with. That's a great consolation to me.'

'Do you mean that Satipy—what *do* you mean?'

'I don't mean anything at all, Renisenb—and please don't start making out that I do. I'm little better than a servant in this house, and it's not my business to give my opinion about things that are nothing to do with me. If you ask me, it's a change for the better, and if it stops at that, well, we'll all do nicely. Now, please, Renisenb, I've got to see that they're marking the date properly on the linen. So careless as they are, these women, always talking and laughing and neglecting their work.'

Unsatisfied, Renisenb watched her dart away into the weaving shed. She herself walked slowly back to the house. Her entry into Satipy's room was unheard, and Satipy sprang round with a cry as Renisenb touched her shoulder.

'Oh you startled me, I thought—'

'Satipy,' said Renisenb. 'What is the matter? Won't you tell me? Yahmose is worried about you and—'

Satipy's fingers flew to her lips. She said, stammering nervously, her eyes wide and frightened: 'Yahmose? What—what did he say?'

'He is anxious. You have been calling out in your sleep—'

'Renisenb!' Satipy caught her by the arm. 'Did I say—What did I say?'

Her eyes seemed dilated with terror.

'Does Yahmose think—what did he tell you?'

'We both think that you are ill—or—or unhappy.'

'Unhappy?' Satipy repeated the word under her breath with a peculiar intonation.

'*Are* you unhappy, Satipy?'

'Perhaps . . . I don't know. It is not that.'

'No. You're frightened, aren't you?'

Satipy stared at her with sudden hostility.

'Why should you say that? Why should I be frightened? What is there to frighten me?'

'I don't know,' said Renisenb. 'But it's true, isn't it?'

With an effort Satipy recovered her old arrogant pose. She tossed her head.

'I'm not afraid of anything—of anyone! How dare you suggest such a thing to me, Renisenb? And I won't have you talking me over with Yahmose. Yahmose and I understand each other.' She paused and then said sharply, 'Nofret is dead—and a good riddance. That's what I say. And you can tell anyone who asks you that that's what I feel about it.'

'Nofret?' Renisenb uttered the name questioningly.

Satipy flew into a passion that made her seem quite like her old self.

'Nofret—Nofret—Nofret! I'm sick of the sound of that name. We don't need to hear it any more in this house—and thank goodness for that.'

Her voice, which had been raised to its old shrill pitch, dropped suddenly as Yahmose entered. He said, with unusual sternness:

'Be quiet, Satipy. If my father heard you, there would be fresh trouble. How can you behave so foolishly?'

If Yahmose's stern and displeased tone was unusual, so too was Satipy's meek collapse. She murmured: 'I am sorry, Yahmose . . . I did not think.'

'Well, be more careful in future! You and Kait made most of the trouble before. You women have no sense!'

Satipy murmured again: 'I am sorry . . .'

Yahmose went out, his shoulders squared, and his walk far more resolute than usual as though the fact of having asserted his authority for once had done him good.

Renisenb went slowly along to old Esa's room. Her grandmother, she felt, might have some helpful counsel.

Esa, however, who was eating grapes with a good deal of relish, refused to take the matter seriously.

'Satipy? Satipy? Why all this fuss about Satipy? Do you all like being bullied and ordered about by her that you make such a to-do because she behaves herself properly for once?'

She spat out the pips of the grape and remarked:

'In any case, it's too good to last—unless Yahmose can keep it up.'

'Yahmose?'

'Yes. I hoped Yahmose had come to his senses at last and given his wife a good beating. It's what she needs—and she's the kind of woman who would probably enjoy it. Yahmose, with his meek, cringing ways, must have been a great trial to her.'

'Yahmose is a dear,' cried Renisenb, indignantly. 'He is kind to everybody—and as gentle as a woman—if women are gentle,' she added, doubtfully.

119

Esa cackled.

'A good afterthought, granddaughter. No, there's nothing gentle about women—or if there is, Isis help them! And there are few women who care for a kind, gentle husband. They'd sooner have a handsome, blustering brute like Sobek—he's the one to take a girl's fancy. Or a smart young fellow like Kameni—hey, Renisenb? The flies in the court-yard don't settle on him for long! He's got a pretty taste in love songs, too. Eh? Hee, hee, hee.'

Renisenb felt her cheeks going red.

'I don't know what you mean,' she said with dignity.

'You all think old Esa doesn't know what's going on! I know all right.' She peered at Renisenb with her semi-blind eyes. 'I know, perhaps, before you do, child. Don't be angry. It's the way of life, Renisenb. Khay was a good brother to you—but he sails his boat now in the Field of Offerings. The sister will find a new brother who spears his fish in our own river—not that Kameni would be much good. A reed pen and a papyrus roll are his fancy. A personable young man, though—with a pretty taste in songs. But for all that I'm not sure he's the man for you. We don't know much about him—he's a Northerner. Imhotep approves of him—but then I've always thought Imhotep was a fool. Anyone can get round him by flattery. Look at Henet!'

'You are quite wrong,' said Renisenb with dignity.

'Very well, then, I'm wrong. Your father is *not* a fool.'

'I didn't mean that. I meant—'

'I know what you meant, child.' Esa grinned. 'But you don't know the real joke. You don't know how good it is to sit at ease like I do, and to be done with all this business of brothers and sisters, and loving and hating. To eat a well-cooked fat quail or a reed bird, and then a cake with honey, and some well-cooked leeks and celery and wash it down with wine from Syria—and have never a care in the world. And look on at all the turmoil and heartaches and know that none of that can affect you any more. To see your son make a fool of himself over a handsome girl, and to see her set the whole place by the ears—it made me laugh, I can tell you! In a way, you know, I liked that girl! She had the devil in her all right—the way she touched them all on the raw. Sobek like a pricked bladder—Ipy made to look a child—Yahmose shamed as a bullied husband. It's like the way you see your face in a pool of water—she made them see just how they looked to the world at large. But why did she hate *you*, Renisenb? Answer me that.'

'Did she hate me?' Renisenb spoke doubtfully. 'I—tried once to be friends.'

'And she'd have none of it? She hated you all right, Renisenb.'

Esa paused and then asked sharply:

'Would it be because of Kameni?'

The colour rose in Renisenb's face: 'Kameni? I do not know what you mean.'

Esa thoughtfully: 'She and Kameni both came from the North, but it was you Kameni watched cross the courtyard.'

Renisenb said abruptly:

'I must go and see to Teti.'

Esa's shrill, amused cackle followed her. Her cheeks hot, Renisenb sped across the courtyard towards the lake.

Kameni called to her from the porch:

'I have made a new song, Renisenb. Stay and hear it.'

She shook her head and hurried on. Her heart was beating angrily. Kameni and Nofret. Nofret and Kameni. Why let old Esa, with her malicious love of mischief, put these ideas into her head? And why should she care?

Anyway what did it matter? She cared nothing for Kameni, nothing at all. An impertinent young man with a laughing voice and shoulders that reminded her of Khay.

Khay . . . Khay.

She repeated his name insistently—but for once no image came before her eyes. Khay was in another world. He was in the Field of Offerings . . .

On the porch Kameni was singing softly:

'*I will say to Ptah: Give me my sister tonight . . .*'

'Renisenb!'

Hori had repeated her name twice before she heard him and turned from her contemplation of the Nile.

'You were lost in thought, Renisenb, what were you thinking about?'

Renisenb said with defiance:

'I was thinking of Khay.'

Hori looked at her for a minute or two—then he smiled:

'I see,' he said.

Renisenb had an uncomfortable feeling that he did see! She said with a sudden rush:

'What happens when you are dead? Does anyone really know? All these texts—all these things that are written on coffins—some of them are so obscure they seem to mean nothing at all. We know that Osiris was killed and that his body was joined together again, and that he wears the white crown, and because of him we need not die—but sometimes, Hori, none of it seems *real*—and it is all so confused . . .'

Hori nodded gently.

'But what really happens after you are dead—that is what I want to know?'

'I cannot tell you, Renisenb. You should ask a priest these questions.'

'He would just give me the usual answers. I want to *know*.'

Hori said gently, 'We shall none of us know until we are dead ourselves . . .'

Renisenb shivered.

'Don't—don't say that!'

'Something has upset you, Renisenb?'

'It was Esa.' She paused and then said, 'Tell me, Hori, did—did Kameni and Nofret know each other well before—before they came here?'

Hori stood quite still for a moment, then as he walked by Renisenb's side, back towards the house, he said, 'I see. So that is how it is . . .'

'What do you mean—"*that is how it is*"? I only asked you a question.'

'To which I do not know the answer. Nofret and Kameni knew each other in the North—how well, I do not know.'

He added gently: 'Does it matter?'

'No, of course not,' said Renisenb. 'It is of no importance at all.'

'Nofret is dead.'

'Dead and embalmed and sealed up in her tomb! And that is that!'

Hori continued calmly:

'And Kameni—does not seem to grieve . . .'

'No,' said Renisenb, struck by this aspect of the question. 'That is true.' She turned to him impulsively. 'Oh Hori, how—how *comforting* a person you are!'

He smiled.

'I mended little Renisenb's lion for her. Now—she has other toys.'

Renisenb skirted the house as they came to it.

'I don't want to go in yet. I feel I hate them all. Oh, not *really*, you understand. But just because I am cross—and impatient and everyone is so *odd*. Can we not go up to your Tomb? It is so nice up there—one is—oh, *above* everything.'

'That is clever of you, Renisenb. That is what I feel. The house and the cultivation and the farming lands—all that is below one, insignificant. One looks beyond all that—to the river—and beyond again—to the whole of Egypt. For very soon now Egypt will be one again—strong and great as she was in the past.'

Renisenb murmured vaguely:

'Oh—does it matter?'

Hori smiled.

'Not to little Renisenb. Only her own lion matters to Renisenb.'

'You are laughing at me, Hori. So it *does* matter to you?'

Hori murmured: 'Why should it? Yes, why should it? I am only a ka-priest's man of business. Why should I care if Egypt is great or small?'

'Look.' Renisenb drew his attention to the cliff above them. 'Yahmose and Satipy have been up to the Tomb. They are coming down now.'

'Yes,' said Hori. 'There were some things to be cleared away, some rolls of linen that the embalmers did not use. Yahmose said he would get Satipy to come up and advise him what to do about them.'

The two of them stood there looking at the two descending the path above.

It came to Renisenb suddenly that they were just approaching the spot from which Nofret must have fallen.

Satipy was ahead. Yahmose a little way behind her.

Suddenly Satipy turned her head to speak to Yahmose. Perhaps, Renisenb thought, she was saying to him that this must be the place where the accident occurred.

And then, suddenly, Satipy stiffened in her tracks. She stood as though frozen, staring back along the path. Her arms went up as though at some dreadful sight or as though to ward off a blow. She cried out something, stumbled, swayed, and then, as Yahmose sprang towards her, she screamed, a scream of terror, and plunged forward off the edge, headlong to the rocks below . . .

Renisenb, her hand to her throat, watched the fall unbelievingly.

Satipy lay, a crumpled mass, just where the body of Nofret had lain.

Rousing herself, Renisenb ran forward to her. Yahmose was calling and running down the path.

Renisenb reached the body of her sister-in-law and bent over it. Satipy's eyes were open, the eyelids fluttering. Her lips were moving, trying to speak. Renisenb bent closer over her. She was appalled by the glazed terror in Satipy's eyes.

Then the dying woman's voice came. It was just a hoarse croak.

'*Nofret . . .*'

Satipy's head fell back. Her jaw dropped.

Hori had turned to meet Yahmose. The two men came up together.

Renisenb turned to her brother.

'What did she call out, up there, before she fell?'

Yahmose's breath was coming in short jerks—he could hardly speak . . .

'She looked past me—*over my shoulder*—as though she saw someone coming along the path—but there was no one—*there was no one there.*'

Hori assented:

'There was no one . . .'

Yahmose's voice dropped to a low, terrified whisper:

'And then she called out—'

'What did she say?' Renisenb demanded, impatiently.

'She said—she said . . .' His voice trembled . . . 'Nofret . . .'

CHAPTER 12

First Month of Summer 12th Day

'So that is what you meant?'

Renisenb flung the words at Hori more as an affirmation than as a question.

She added softly under her breath with growing comprehension and horror:

'It was Satipy who killed Nofret . . .'

Sitting with her chin supported by her hands in the entrance to Hori's little rock chamber next to the Tomb, Renisenb stared down at the valley below.

She thought dreamily how true the words were she had uttered yesterday—(was it really only such a short time ago?—) From up here the house below and the busy hurrying figures had no more significance nor meaning than an ants' nest.

Only the sun, majestic in power, shining overhead—only the slim streak of pale silver that was the Nile in this morning light—only these were eternal and enduring. Khay had died, and Nofret and Satipy—and some day she and Hori would die. But Ra would still rule the heavens

127

and travel by night in his barque through the Underworld to the dawning of the next day. And the river would still flow, flow from beyond Elephantine and down past Thebes and past the village and to lower Egypt where Nofret had lived and been gay and light of heart, and on to the great waters and so away from Egypt altogether.

Satipy and Nofret . . .

Renisenb pursued her thoughts aloud since Hori had not answered her.

'You see, I was so sure that Sobek—'

She broke off.

Hori said thoughtfully: 'The preconceived idea.'

'And yet it was stupid of me,' Renisenb went on. 'Henet told me, or more or less told me, that Satipy had gone walking this way and she said that Nofret had come up here. I ought to have seen how obvious it was that Satipy had followed Nofret—that they had met on the path—and that Satipy had thrown her down. She had said, only a short while before, that she was a better man than any of my brothers.'

Renisenb broke off and shivered.

'And when I met her—' she resumed, 'I should have known then. She was quite different—she was frightened. She tried to persuade me to turn back with her. She didn't want me to find Nofret's body. I must have been blind not to realize the truth. But I was so full of fear about Sobek . . .'

'I know. It was seeing him kill that snake.'

Renisenb agreed eagerly.

'Yes, that was it. And then I had a dream . . . Poor Sobek—how I have misjudged him. As you say, *threatening*

128

is not *doing*. Sobek has always been full of boastful talk. It was Satipy who was always bold and ruthless and not afraid of action. And then ever since—the way she has gone about like a ghost—it has puzzled us all—why did we not think of the true explanation?'

She added, with a quick upward glance:

'But you did?'

'For some time,' said Hori, 'I have felt convinced that the clue to the truth of Nofret's death was in Satipy's extraordinary change of character. It was so remarkable that there had to be something to account for it.'

'And yet you said nothing?'

'How could I, Renisenb? What could I ever *prove*?'

'No, of course not.'

'Proofs must be solid brick walls of fact.'

'Yet once you said,' Renisenb argued, 'that people didn't really change. But now you admit that Satipy *did* change.'

Hori smiled at her.

'You should argue in the Nomarch's courts. No, Renisenb, what I said was true enough—people are always themselves. Satipy, like Sobek, was all bold words and talk. She, indeed, might go on from talk to action—but I think she is one of those who cannot know a thing or what it is like until it has happened. In her life up to that particular day, she had never had anything to *fear*. When fear came, it took her unawares. She learned then that courage is the resolution to face the unforeseen—and she had not got that courage.'

Renisenb murmured in a low voice:

'*When fear* came . . . Yes, that is what has been with us

ever since Nofret died. Satipy has carried it in her face for us all to see. It was there, staring from her eyes when she died . . . when she said "Nofret . . ." It was as though she saw—'

Renisenb stopped herself. She turned her face to Hori, her eyes wide with a question. 'Hori, what did she see? There on the path. *We* saw nothing! There *was* nothing.'

'Not for us—no.'

'But for her? It was Nofret she saw—Nofret come to take her revenge. But Nofret is dead and her tomb is sealed. What then did she see?'

'The picture that her own mind showed her.'

'You are sure? Because if not—'

'Yes, Renisenb, if not?'

'Hori—' Renisenb stretched out her hand. 'Is it ended now? Now that Satipy is dead? Is it truly ended?'

He held her hand in both of his in a comforting clasp.

'Yes, yes, Renisenb—surely. And you at least need not be afraid.'

'Renisenb murmured under her breath:

'But Esa says that Nofret hated me . . .'

'Nofret hated *you*?'

'Esa says so.'

'Nofret was good at hating,' said Hori. 'Sometimes I think she hated every person in this house. But you at least did nothing against her.'

'No—no, that is true.'

'And therefore, Renisenb, there is nothing in *your* mind to rise up against you in judgement.'

'You mean, Hori, that if I were to walk down this path

alone—at sunset—at that same time when Nofret died—
and if I were to turn my head—I should see nothing? I
should be safe?'

'You will be safe, Renisenb, because if you walk down
the path, I will walk with you and no harm shall come to
you.'

But Renisenb frowned and shook her head.

'No, Hori. I will walk alone.'

'But why, little Renisenb? Will you not be afraid?'

'Yes,' said Renisenb, 'I think I shall be afraid. But all the
same that is what has to be done. They are all trembling
and shaking in the house and running to the Temples to
buy amulets and crying out that it is not well to walk on
this path at the hour of sundown. But it was not magic
that made Satipy sway and fall—it was fear—fear because
of an evil thing that she had done. For it is evil to take
away life from someone who is young and strong and who
enjoys living. But I have not done any evil thing, and so
even if Nofret did hate me, her hate cannot harm me. That
is what I believe. And anyway if one is to live always in
fear it would be better to die—so I will overcome fear.'

'These are brave words, Renisenb.'

'They are perhaps rather braver than I feel, Hori.' She
smiled up at him. She rose to her feet. 'But it has been
good to say them.'

Hori rose and stood beside her. 'I shall remember these
words of yours, Renisenb. Yes, and the way you threw
back your head when you said them. They show the courage
and the truth that I have always felt was in your heart.'

He took her hand in his.

'Look, Renisenb. Look out from here across the valley to the river and beyond. That is Egypt, our land. Broken by war and strife for many long years, divided into petty kingdoms, but now—very soon—to come together and form once more a united land—Upper and Lower Egypt once again welded into one—I hope and believe to recover her former greatness! In those days, Egypt will need men and women of heart and courage—women such as you, Renisenb. It is not men like Imhotep, forever preoccupied with his own narrow gains and losses, nor men like Sobek, idle and boastful, nor boys like Ipy who thinks only of what he can gain for himself, no, nor even conscientious, honest sons like Yahmose whom Egypt will need in that hour. Sitting here, literally amongst the dead, reckoning up gains and losses, casting accounts, I have come to see gains that cannot be reckoned in terms of wealth, and losses that are more damaging than loss of a crop . . . I look at the river and I see the life blood of Egypt that has existed before we lived and that will exist after we die . . . Life and death, Renisenb, are not of such great account. I am only Hori, Imhotep's man of business, but when I look out over Egypt I know a peace—yes, and an exultation that I would not exchange to be Governor of the Province. Do you understand at all what I mean, Renisenb?'

'I think so, Hori—a little. You are different from the others down there—I have known that for some time. And sometimes when I am with you here, I can feel what you feel—but dimly—not very clearly. But I do know what you mean. When I am *here* the things down *there*,' she pointed, 'do not seem to matter any longer. The quarrels

132

and the hatreds and the incessant bustle and fuss. Here one escapes from all that.'

She paused, her brow puckering, and went on, stammering a little.

'Sometimes I—I am glad to have escaped. And yet—I do not know—there is something—down there—that calls me back.'

Hori dropped her hand and stepped back a pace.

He said gently:

'Yes—I see—Kameni singing in the courtyard.'

'What do you mean, Hori? I was not thinking of Kameni.'

'You may not have been thinking of him. But all the same, Renisenb, I think it is his songs that you are hearing without knowing it.'

Renisenb stared at him, her brow puckered.

'What extraordinary things you say, Hori. One could not possibly hear him singing up here. It is much too far away.'

Hori sighed gently and shook his head. The amusement in his eyes puzzled her. She felt a little angry and bewildered because she could not understand.

CHAPTER 13

First Month of Summer 23rd Day

'Can I speak with you a minute, Esa?'

Esa peered sharply towards Henet who stood in the doorway of the room, an ingratiating smile upon her face.

'What is it?' the old woman asked sharply.

'It's nothing really—at least I don't suppose so—but I thought I'd just like to ask—'

Esa cut her short. 'Come in, then, come in. And you—' she tapped the little black slave girl, who was threading beads, on the shoulder with her stick—'go to the kitchen. Get me some olives—and make me a drink of pomegranate juice.'

The little girl ran off and Esa beckoned Henet impatiently.

'It's just this, Esa.'

Esa peered down at the article Henet was holding out to her. It was a small jewel box with a sliding lid, the top fastened with two buttons.

'What about it?'

'It's *hers*. And I found it now—in her room.'

134

'Who are you talking about? Satipy?'

'No, no, Esa. *The other.*'

'Nofret, you mean? What of it?'

'All her jewels and her toilet vases and her perfume jars—everything—was buried with her.'

Esa twirled the string from the buttons and opened the box. In it was a string of small carnelian beads and half of a green glazed amulet which had been broken in two.

'Pooh,' said Esa. 'Nothing much here. It must have been overlooked.'

'The embalmers' men took everything away.'

'Embalmers' men aren't any more reliable than anyone else. They forgot this.'

'I tell you, Esa—this wasn't in the room when last I looked in.'

Esa looked up sharply at Henet.

'What are you trying to make out? That Nofret has come back from the Underworld and is here in the house? You're not really a fool, Henet, though you sometimes like to pretend you're one. What pleasure do you get from spreading these silly magical tales?'

Henet was shaking her head portentously.

'We all know what happened to Satipy—and *why*!'

'Maybe we do,' said Esa. 'And maybe some of us knew it before! Eh, Henet? I've always had an idea you knew more about how Nofret came to her death than the rest of us.'

'Oh, Esa, surely you wouldn't think for a moment—'

Esa cut her short.

'What wouldn't I think? I'm not afraid of thinking,

Henet. I've seen Satipy creeping about the house for the last two months looking frightened to death—and it's occurred to me since yesterday that someone might have been holding the knowledge over her head—threatening maybe to tell Yahmose—or Imhotep himself—'

Henet burst into a shrill clamour of protestations and exclamations. Esa closed her eyes and leaned back in her chair.

'I don't suppose for a moment you'd ever admit you did such a thing. I'm not expecting you to.'

'Why should I? That's what I ask you—why should I?'

'I've not the least idea,' said Esa. 'You do a lot of things, Henet, for which I've never been able to find a satisfactory reason.'

'I suppose you think I was trying to make her bribe me to silence. I swear by the Nine Gods of the Ennead—'

'Do not trouble the Gods. You're honest enough, Henet— as honesty goes. And it may be that you knew nothing about how Nofret came to her death. But you know most things that go on in this house. And if I were going to do any swearing myself, I'd swear that you put this box in Nofret's room yourself—though why I can't imagine. But there's some reason behind it . . . You can deceive Imhotep with your tricks, but you can't deceive me. And don't *whine*! I'm an old woman and I cannot stand people whining. Go and whine to Imhotep. He seems to like it, though Rē alone knows why!'

'I will take the box to Imhotep and tell him—'

'I'll hand the box to him myself. Be off with you, Henet, and stop spreading these silly superstitious tales. The house is a more peaceful place without Satipy. Nofret dead has done more for us than Nofret living. But now that the debt is paid, let everyone return to their everyday tasks.'

'What is all this?' Imhotep demanded as he came fussily into Esa's room a few minutes later. 'Henet is deeply distressed. She came to me with the tears running down her face. Why nobody in the house can show that devoted woman the most ordinary kindness—'

Esa, unmoved, gave a cackle of laughter.

Imhotep went on:

'You have accused her, I understand, of stealing a box—a jewel box.'

'Is that what she told you? I did nothing of the sort. Here is the box. It seems it was found in Nofret's room.'

Imhotep took it from her.

'Ah yes, it is one I gave her.' He opened it. 'H'm, nothing much inside. Very careless of the embalmers not to have included it with the rest of her personal belongings. Considering the prices Ipi and Montu charge, one could at least expect no carelessness. Well, this all seems to me a great fuss about nothing—'

'Quite so.'

'I will give the box to Kait—no, to Renisenb. She always behaved with courtesy towards Nofret.'

He sighed.

'How impossible it seems for a man to get any peace. These women—endless tears or else quarrels and bickerings.'

'Ah well, Imhotep, there is at least one woman less now!'

'Yes, indeed. My poor Yahmose! All the same, Esa—I feel that—er—it may be all for the best. Satipy bore healthy children, it is true, but she was in many ways a most unsatisfactory wife. Yahmose, of course, gave in to her far too much. Well, well, all that is over now. I must say that I have been much pleased with Yahmose's behaviour of late. He seems much more self-reliant—less timid—and his judgement on several points has been excellent—quite excellent . . .'

'He was always a good, obedient boy.'

'Yes, yes—but inclined to be slow and somewhat afraid of responsibility.'

Esa said drily: 'Responsibility is a thing you have never allowed him to have!'

'Well, all that will be changed now. I am arranging a deed of association and partnership. It will be signed in a few days' time. I am associating with myself all my three sons.'

'Surely not Ipy?'

'He would be hurt to be left out. Such a dear, warm-hearted lad.'

'There is certainly nothing slow about *him*,' observed Esa.

'As you say. And Sobek too—I have been displeased with him in the past, but he has really turned over a new leaf of late. He no longer idles his time away, and he defers more to my judgement and to that of Yahmose.'

'This is indeed a hymn of praise,' said Esa. 'Well, Imhotep, I must say that I think you are doing the right thing. It was bad policy to make your sons discontented. But I still think that Ipy is too young for what you propose. It is ridiculous to give a boy of that age a definite position. What hold will you have over him?'

'There is something in that, certainly.' Imhotep looked thoughtful.

Then he roused himself.

'I must go. There are a thousand things to see to. The embalmers are here—there are all the arrangements to make for Satipy's burial. These deaths are costly—very costly. And following so quickly one upon the other!'

'Oh well,' said Esa consolingly, 'we'll hope this is the last of them—until my time comes!'

'You will live many years yet, I hope, my dear mother.'

'I'm sure you hope so,' said Esa with a grin. 'No economy over me, if you please! It wouldn't look well! I shall want a good deal of equipment to amuse me in the other world. Plenty of food and drink and a lot of models of slaves—a richly ornamented gaming board, perfume sets and cosmetics, and I insist on the most expensive canopic jars—the alabaster ones.'

'Yes, yes, of course.' Imhotep changed his position nervously from one foot to the other. 'Naturally all respect will be paid when the sad day comes. I must confess that I feel rather differently about Satipy. One does not want a scandal, but really, *in the circumstances*—'

Imhotep did not finish his sentence but hurried away.

Esa smiled sardonically as she realized that that one phrase 'in the circumstances' was the nearest Imhotep would ever get towards admitting that an accident did not fully describe the way his valued concubine met her death.

CHAPTER 14

First Month of Summer 25th Day

With the return of the members of the family from the Nomarch's court, the deed of association duly ratified, a general spirit of hilarity was felt. The exception was undoubtedly Ipy who had, at the last moment, been excluded from participation on the ground of his extreme youth. He was sullen in consequence and purposefully absented himself from the house.

Imhotep, in excellent spirits, called for a pitcher of wine to be brought out on to the porch where it was placed in the big wine stand.

'You shall drink, my son,' he declared, clapping Yahmose on the shoulder. 'Forget for the moment your sorrow in bereavement. Let us think only of the good days that are to come.'

Imhotep, Yahmose, Sobek and Hori drank the toast. Then word was brought that an ox had been stolen, and all four men went hurriedly off to investigate the matter.

When Yahmose re-entered the courtyard, an hour later, he was tired and hot. He went to where the wine jar still stood in the stand. He dipped a bronze cup into it and sat down on the porch, gently sipping the wine. A little later Sobek came striding in and exclaimed with pleasure.

'Ha,' he said. 'Now for more wine! Let us drink to our future which is at last well assured. Undoubtedly this is a joyful day for *us*, Yahmose!'

Yahmose agreed.

'Yes, indeed. It will make life easier in every way.'

'You are always so moderate in your feelings, Yahmose.'

Sobek laughed as he spoke and dipping a cup in the wine, he tossed it off, smacking his lips as he put it down.

'Let us see now whether my father will be as much of a stick in the mud as ever, or whether I shall be able to convert him to up-to-date methods.'

'I should go slowly if I were you,' Yahmose counselled. 'You are always so hot-headed.'

Sobek smiled at his brother affectionately. He was in high good humour.

'Old slow-and-sure,' he said, scoffingly.

Yahmose smiled, not at all put out.

'It is the best way in the end. Besides, my father has been very good to us. We must do nothing to cause him worry.'

Sobek looked at him curiously.

'You are really fond of our father? You are an affectionate creature, Yahmose! Now I—I care for nobody—for nobody, that is, but Sobek, long life to him!'

He took another draught of wine.

'Be careful,' Yahmose said warningly. 'You have eaten little today. Sometimes, then, when one drinks wine—'

He broke off with a sudden contortion of the lips.

'What is the matter, Yahmose?'

'Nothing—a sudden pain—I, it is nothing . . .'

But he raised a hand to wipe his forehead which was suddenly bedewed with moisture.

'You do not look well.'

'I was quite all right just now.'

'So long as nobody has poisoned the wine.' Sobek laughed at his own words and stretched out his arm towards the jar. Then, in the very act, his arm stiffened, his body bent forward in a sudden spasm of agony . . .

'Yahmose,' he gasped. 'Yahmose . . . I—too . . .'

Yahmose, slipping forward, was bent double. A half stifled cry came from him.

Sobek was now contorted with pain. He raised his voice.

'Help. Send for a physician—a physician . . .'

Henet came running out of the house.

'You called? What was it that you said? What is it?'

Her alarmed cries brought others.

The two brothers were both groaning with pain.

Yahmose said faintly:

'The wine—poison—send for a physician . . .'

Henet uttered a shrill cry:

'More misfortune. In truth this house is accursed. Quick! Hurry! Send to the Temple for the Divine Father Mersu who is a skilled physician of great experience.'

Imhotep paced up and down the central hall of the house. His fine linen robe was soiled and limp, he had neither bathed nor changed. His face was drawn with worry and fear.

From the back of the house came a low sound of keening and weeping—the women's contribution to the catastrophe that had overrun the household—Henet's voice led the mourners.

From a room at the side, the voice of the physician and priest Mersu was heard raised as he strove over the inert body of Yahmose. Renisenb, stealing quietly out of the women's quarters into the central hall, was drawn by the sound. Her feet took her to the open doorway and she paused there, feeling a healing balm in the sonorous words that the priest was reciting.

'*Oh Isis, great of magic, loose thou me, release thou me from all things bad, evil and red, from the stroke of a God, from the stroke of a Goddess, from dead man or dead woman, from a male foe, or a female foe who may oppose himself to me . . .*'

A faint sigh came fluttering from Yahmose's lips.

In her heart Renisenb joined in the prayer.

'Oh Isis—oh great Isis—save him—save my brother Yahmose—Thou who art great of magic . . .'

Thoughts passed confusedly through her mind, raised there by the words of the incantation.

'*From all things bad, evil and red . . . That* is what has been the matter with us here in this house—yes, red thoughts, angry thoughts—the anger of a dead woman.'

She spoke within the confines of her thoughts, directly addressing the person in her mind.

'It was not Yahmose who harmed you, Nofret—and

Agatha Christie

though Satipy was his wife, you cannot hold him responsible for her actions—he never had any control over her—no one had. Satipy who harmed you is dead. Is that not enough? Sobek is dead—Sobek who only spoke against you, yet never actually harmed you. Oh Isis, do not let Yahmose also die—save him from the vengeful hatred of Nofret.'

Imhotep, pacing distractedly up and down, looked up and saw his daughter and his face relaxed with affection.

'Come here, Renisenb, dear child.'

She ran to him and he put his arms around her.

'Oh, father, what do they say?'

Imhotep said heavily: 'They say that in Yahmose's case there is hope. Sobek—you know?'

'Yes, yes. Have you not heard us wailing?'

'He died at dawn,' said Imhotep. 'Sobek, my strong, handsome son.' His voice faltered and broke.

'Oh it is wicked, cruel—could nothing be done?'

'All was done that could be. Potions forcing him to vomit. Administration of the juice of potent herbs. Sacred amulets were applied and mighty incantations spoken. All was of no avail. Mersu is a skilled physician. If he could not save my son—then it was the will of the Gods that he should not be saved.'

The priest physician's voice rose in a final high chant and he came out from the chamber, wiping the perspiration from his forehead.

'Well?' Imhotep accosted him eagerly.

The physician said gravely: 'By the favour of Isis your son will live. He is weak, but the crisis of the poison has passed. The evil influence is on the wane.'

He went on, slightly altering his tone to a more everyday intonation.

'It is fortunate that Yahmose drank much less of the poisoned wine. He sipped his wine whereas it seems your son Sobek tossed it off at a draught.'

Imhotep groaned.

'You have there the difference between them. Yahmose timid, cautious and slow in his approach to everything. Even eating and drinking. Sobek, always given to excess, generous, free-handed—alas! imprudent.'

Then he added sharply:

'And the wine was definitely poisoned?'

'There is no doubt of that, Imhotep. The residue was tested by my young assistants—of the animals treated with it, all died more or less swiftly.'

'And yet I who had drunk the same wine not an hour earlier have felt no ill effects.'

'It was doubtless not poisoned at that time—the poison was added afterwards.'

Imhotep struck the palm of one hand with his other hand clenched into a fist.

'No one,' he declared, 'no one living would dare to poison my sons here under my roof! Such a thing is impossible. No *living* person, I say!'

Mersu inclined his head slightly. His face became inscrutable.

'Of that, Imhotep, you are the best judge.'

Imhotep stood scratching nervously behind his ear.

'There is a tale I would like you to hear,' he said abruptly. He clapped his hands and as a servant ran in, he called:

145

'Bring the herd boy here.'

He turned back to Mersu, saying:

'This is a boy whose wits are not of the best. He takes in what people say to him with difficulty and he has not full possession of his faculties. Nevertheless he has eyes and his eyesight is good, and he is moreover devoted to my son Yahmose who has been gentle with him and kindly to his infirmity.'

The servant came back, dragging by the hand a thin, almost black-skinned boy, clad in a loin-cloth, with slightly squinting eyes and a frightened, witless face.

'Speak,' said Imhotep sharply. 'Repeat what you told me just now.'

The boy hung his head, his fingers began kneading the cloth round his waist.

'Speak,' shouted Imhotep.

Esa came hobbling in, supported by her stick and peering with her dim eyes.

'You are terrifying the child. Here, Renisenb, give him this jujube. There, boy, tell us what you saw.'

The boy gazed from one to the other of them.

Esa prompted him.

'It was yesterday, as you passed the door of the court-yard—you saw—what did you see?'

The boy shook his head, glancing sideways. He murmured:

'Where is my Lord Yahmose?'

The priest spoke with authority and kindliness:

'It is the wish of your Lord Yahmose that you tell us your tale. Have no fear. No one will hurt you.'

146

A gleam of light passed over the boy's face. 'My Lord Yahmose has been good to me. I will do what he wishes.'

He paused. Imhotep seemed about to break out, but a look from the physician restrained him.

Suddenly the boy spoke, nervously, in a quick gabble, and with a look from side to side as he spoke, as though he was afraid that some unseen presence would overhear him.

'It was the little donkey—protected by Seth and always up to mischief. I ran after him with my stick. He went past the big gate of the courtyard, and I looked in through the gate at the house. There was no one on the porch, but there was a wine-stand there. And then a woman, a lady of the house, came out upon the porch from the house. She walked to the wine jar and she held out her hands over it and then—and then—she went back into the house, I think. I do not know. For I heard footsteps and turned and saw in the distance my Lord Yahmose coming back from the fields. So I went on seeking the little donkey, and my Lord Yahmose went into the courtyard.'

'And you did not warn him,' cried Imhotep, angrily. 'You said nothing.'

The boy cried out, 'I did not know anything was wrong. I saw nothing but the lady standing there smiling down as she spread out her hands over the wine jar . . . I saw nothing . . .'

'Who was this lady, boy?' asked the priest.

With a vacant expression the boy shook his head.

'I do not know. She must have been one of the ladies of the house. I do not know them. I have the herds at the far end of the cultivation. She wore a dress of dyed linen.'

Renisenb started.

'A servant, perhaps?' suggested the priest, watching the boy.

The boy shook his head positively.

'She was not a servant . . . She had a wig on her head and she wore jewels—a servant does not wear jewels.'

'Jewels?' demanded Imhotep. 'What jewels?'

The boy replied eagerly and confidently as though at last he had overcome his fear and was quite sure of what he was saying.

'Three strings of beads with gold lions hanging from them in front . . .'

Esa's stick clattered to the floor. Imhotep uttered a stifled cry.

Mersu said threateningly: 'If you are lying, boy—'

'It is the truth. I swear it is the truth.' The boy's voice rose shrill and clear.

From the side chamber where the ill man lay, Yahmose called feebly: 'What is all this?'

The boy darted through the open door and crouched down by the couch on which Yahmose lay.

'Master, they will torture me.'

'No, no.' Yahmose turned his head with difficulty on the curved, wooden headrest. 'Do not let the child be hurt. He is simple, but honest. Promise me.'

'Of course, of course,' said Imhotep. 'There is no need. It is clear the boy has told all that he knows—and I do not think he is inventing. Be off with you, child, but do not return to the far herds. Stay near the house so that we can summon you again if we need you.'

The boy rose to his feet. He bent a reluctant glance upon Yahmose.

'You are ill, Lord Yahmose?'

Yahmose smiled faintly.

'Have no fear. I am not going to die. Go now—and be obedient to what you have been told.'

Smiling happily now, the boy went off. The priest examined Yahmose's eyes and felt the rate at which the blood was coursing under the skin. Then, recommending him to sleep, he went with the others out into the central hall again.

He said to Imhotep:

'You recognize the description the boy gave?'

Imhotep nodded. His deep, bronze cheeks showed a sickly plum colour.

Renisenb said: 'Only Nofret ever wore a dress of dyed linen. It was a new fashion she brought with her from the cities in the North. But those dresses were buried with her.'

Imhotep said:

'And the three strings of beads with the lions' heads in gold were what I gave her. There is no other such ornament in the house. It was costly and unusual. All her jewellery, with the exception of a trumpery string of carnelian beads, was buried with her and is sealed in her tomb.'

He flung out his arms.

'What persecution—what vindictiveness is this! My concubine whom I treated well, to whom I paid all honour, whom I buried with the proper rites, sparing no expense. I have eaten and drunk with her in friendship—to that all can bear witness. She had had nothing of which to complain—I did indeed more for her than would have been considered right and fitting. I was prepared to favour her to the detriment of my sons who were born to me. Why, then, should she thus come back from the dead to persecute me and my family?'

Mersu said gravely:

'It seems that it is not against you personally that the dead woman wishes evil. The wine when you drank it was harmless. Who in your family did injury to your dead concubine?'

'A woman who is dead,' Imhotep answered shortly.

'I see. You mean the wife of your son Yahmose?'

'Yes.' Imhotep paused, then broke out: 'But what can be done, Reverend Father? How can we counteract this malice? Oh, evil day when I first took the woman into my house.'

'An evil day, indeed,' said Kait in a deep voice, coming forward from the entrance to the women's quarters.

Her eyes were heavy with the tears she had shed, and her plain face had a strength and resolution which made it noticeable. Her voice, deep and hoarse, was shaken with anger.

'It was an evil day when you brought Nofret here, Imhotep, to destroy the cleverest and most handsome of your sons! She has brought death to Satipy and death to my Sobek, and Yahmose has only narrowly escaped. Who will be next? Will she spare even children—she who struck my little Ankh? Something must be *done*, Imhotep!'

'Something *must* be done,' Imhotep echoed, looking imploringly at the priest.

The latter nodded his head with calm assumption.

'There are ways and means, Imhotep. Once we are sure

of our facts, we can go ahead. I have in mind your dead wife, Ashayet. She was a woman of influential family. She can invoke powerful interests in the Land of the Dead, who can intervene on your behalf and against whom the woman Nofret will have no power. We must take counsel together.'

Kait gave a short laugh.

'Do not wait too long. Men are always the same—Yes, even priests! Everything must be done according to law and precedent. But I say, act quickly—or there will be more dead beneath this roof.'

She turned and went out.

'An excellent woman,' murmured Imhotep. 'A devoted mother to her children, a dutiful wife—but her manners, sometimes, are hardly what they should be—to the head of the house. Naturally at such a time I forgive her. We are all distraught. We hardly know what we are doing.'

He clasped his hands to his head.

'Some of us seldom do know what we are doing,' remarked Esa.

Imhotep shot an annoyed glance at her. The physician prepared to take his leave and Imhotep went out with him on to the porch, receiving instructions for the care of the sick man.

Renisenb, left behind, looked inquiringly at her grandmother.

Esa was sitting very still. She was frowning and the expression on her face was so curious that Renisenb asked timidly:

'What is it that you are thinking, grandmother?'

'Thinking is the word, Renisenb. Such curious things are happening in this house that it is very necessary for someone to think.'

'They are terrible,' said Renisenb with a shiver. 'They frighten me.'

'They frighten *me*,' said Esa. 'But not perhaps for the same reason.'

With the old familiar gesture, she pushed the wig on her head askew.

'But Yahmose will not die now,' said Renisenb. 'He will live.'

Esa nodded.

'Yes, a Master Physician reached him in time. On another occasion, though, he may not be so lucky.'

'You think—there will be other happenings like this?'

'I think that Yahmose and you and Ipy—and perhaps Kait too, had better be very careful indeed what you eat and drink. See always that a slave tastes it first.'

'And you, grandmother?'

Esa smiled her sardonic smile.

'I, Renisenb, am an old woman, and I love life as only the old can, savouring every hour, every minute that is left to them. Of you all I have the best chance of life—because I shall be more careful than any of you.'

'And my father? Surely Nofret would wish no evil to my father?'

'Your father? I do not know . . . No, I do not know. I cannot as yet see clearly. Tomorrow, when I have thought about it all, I must speak once more with that herd boy. There was something about his story—'

She broke off, frowning. Then, with a sigh, she rose to her feet, and helping herself with her stick, limped slowly back to her own quarters.

Renisenb went into her brother's room. He was sleeping and she crept out again softly. After a moment's hesitation she went to Kait's quarters. She stood in the doorway unnoticed, watching Kait sing one of the children to sleep. Kait's face was calm and placid again—she looked so much as usual that for a moment Renisenb felt that the whole tragic occurrences of the last twenty-four hours were a dream.

She turned slowly away and went to her own apartment. On a table, amongst her own cosmetic boxes and jars, was the little jewel case that had belonged to Nofret.

Renisenb picked it up and stood looking at it as it lay on the palm of her hand. Nofret had touched it, had held it—it was her possession.

And again a wave of pity swept over Renisenb, allied to that queer sense of understanding. Nofret had been unhappy. As she had held this little box in her hand perhaps she had deliberately forced that unhappiness into malice and hatred . . . and even now that hatred was unabated . . . was still seeking revenge . . . Oh no, surely not—surely not!

Almost mechanically, Renisenb twisted the two buttons and slid back the lid. The carnelian beads were there and the broken amulet and *something else* . . .

Her heart beating violently, Renisenb drew out a necklace of gold beads with gold lions in front . . .

153

CHAPTER 15

First Month of Summer 30th Day

The finding of the necklace frightened Renisenb badly.

On the impulse of the minute she replaced it quickly in the jewel box, slid home the lid and tied the string round the buttons again. Her instinct was to conceal her discovery. She even glanced fearfully behind her to make sure that no one had watched what she had been doing.

She passed a sleepless night, twisting to and fro uneasily and settling and resettling her head on the curved wooden headrest of her bed.

By the morning she had decided that she must confide in someone. She could not bear the weight of that disturbing discovery alone. Twice in the night she had started up, wondering if, perhaps, she might perceive Nofret's figure standing menacingly by her side. But there was nothing to be seen.

Taking the lion necklace from the jewel box, Renisenb hid it in the folds of her linen dress. She had only just done so when Henet came bustling in. Her eyes were bright and sharp with the pleasure of having fresh news to impart.

'Just imagine, Renisenb, isn't it terrible? That boy—the herd boy, you know—fast asleep this morning out by the cornbins and everyone shaking him and yelling in his ear—and now it seems that he'll never wake again. It's as though he'd drunk the poppy juice—and maybe he did—but if so who gave it to him? Nobody here, that I'll be bound. And it's not likely he'd take it himself. Oh, we might have known how it would be yesterday.' Henet's hand went to one of the many amulets she wore. 'Amūn protect us against the evil spirits of the dead! The boy told what he saw. He told how he saw her. And so she came back and gave him poppy juice to close his eyes for ever. Oh, She's very powerful, that Nofret! She's been abroad, you know, out of Egypt. I dare swear she got to know all sorts of outlandish primitive magic. We're not safe in this house—none of us are safe. Your father should give several bulls to Amūn—a whole herd if necessary— this isn't a time for economy. We've got to protect ourselves. We must appeal to your mother—that's what Imhotep is planning to do. The Priest Mersu says so. A solemn Letter to the Dead. Hori is busy now drawing up the terms of it. Your father was for addressing it to Nofret—appealing to her. You know: "Most excellent Nofret, what evil thing have I ever done to you—" etc. But as the Divine Father Mersu pointed out, it needs stronger measures than *that*. Now your mother, Ashayet, was a great lady. Her mother's brother was the Nomarch and her brother was Chief Butler to the Vizier of Thebes. If it's once brought to *her* knowledge, she'll see to it that a mere concubine isn't allowed to destroy her own children! Oh yes, we'll get justice done. As I say, Hori is drawing up the plea to her now.'

It had been Renisenb's intention to seek out Hori and tell him about her finding of the lion necklace. But if Hori were busy with the priests at the Temple of Isis it was hopeless to think of trying to get hold of him alone.

Should she go to her father? Dissatisfied, Renisenb shook her head. Her old childish belief in her father's omnipotence had quite passed away. She realized now how quickly in times of crisis he went to pieces—a fussy pomposity replacing any real strength. If Yahmose were not ill, she could have told him, though she doubted if he would have any very practical counsels to offer. He would probably insist on the matter being laid before Imhotep.

And that, Renisenb felt with increasing urgency, was at all costs to be avoided. The first thing Imhotep would do would be to blazon the whole thing abroad, and Renisenb had a strong instinct for keeping it secret—though for what reason she would have been hard put to it to say.

No, it was Hori's advice she wanted. Hori would, as always, know the right thing to do. He would take the necklace from her and at the same time take her worry and perplexity away. He would look at her with those kind grave eyes and instantly she would feel that now all was well . . .

For a moment Renisenb was tempted to confide in Kait—but Kait was unsatisfactory, she never listened properly. Perhaps if one got her away from her children—no, it wouldn't do. Kait was nice, but stupid.

Renisenb thought: 'There is Kameni . . . and there is my grandmother.'

Kameni . . .? There was something pleasurable in the thought of telling Kameni. She could see his face quite clearly in her thoughts—its expression changing from a merry challenge to interest—to apprehension on her behalf . . . Or would it not be on her behalf?

Why this insidious lurking suspicion that Nofret and Kameni had been closer friends than had appeared on the surface? Because Kameni had helped Nofret in her campaign of detaching Imhotep from his family? He had protested that he could not help himself—but was that true? It was an easy thing to say. Everything Kameni said sounded easy and natural and right. His laugh was so gay that you wanted to laugh too. The swing of his body was so graceful as he walked—the turn of his head on those smooth bronze shoulders—his eyes that looked at you—that looked at you—Renisenb's thoughts broke off confusedly. Kameni's eyes were not like Hori's eyes, safe and kind. They demanded, they challenged.

Renisenb's thoughts had brought blood into her cheeks and a sparkle into her eye. But she decided that she would not tell Kameni about the finding of Nofret's necklace. No, she would go to Esa. Esa had impressed her yesterday. Old as she was, the old woman had a grasp of things and a shrewd practical sense that was unshared by anyone else in the family.

Renisenb thought: 'She is old. But she will know.'

At the first mention of the necklace, Esa glanced quickly round, placed a finger to her lips and held out her hand.

Renisenb fumbled in her dress, drew out the necklace and laid it in Esa's hand. Esa held it for a moment close to her dim eyes, then stowed it away in her dress. She said in a low, authoritative voice:

'No more now. Talking in this house is talking to a hundred ears. I have lain awake most of the night thinking, and there is much that must be done.'

'My father and Hori have gone to the Temple of Isis to confer with the Priest Mersu on the drawing up of a petition to my mother for her intervention.'

'I know. Well, let your father concern himself with the spirits of the dead. My thoughts deal with the things of this world. When Hori returns, bring him here to me. There are things that must be said and discussed—and Hori I can trust.'

'Hori will know what to do,' said Renisenb happily.

Esa looked at her curiously.

'You go often to see him at the Tomb, do you not? What do you talk about, you and Hori?'

Renisenb shook her head vaguely.

'Oh, the river—and Egypt—and the way the light changes and the colours of the sand below and the rocks . . . But very often we do not talk at all. I just sit there and it is peaceful, with no scolding voices and no crying children and no bustle of coming and going. I can think my own thoughts and Hori does not interrupt them. And then, sometimes, I look up and find him watching me and we both smile . . . I can be happy up there.'

Esa said slowly:

'You are lucky, Renisenb. You have found the happiness

that is inside everybody's own heart. To most women happiness means coming and going, busied over small affairs. It is care for one's children and laughter and conversation and quarrels with other women and alternate love and anger with a man. It is made up of small things strung together like beads on a string.'

'Has your life been like that, grandmother?'

'Most of it. But now that I am old and sit much alone and my sight is dim and I walk with difficulty—then I realize that there is a life within as well as a life without. But I am too old now to learn the true way of it—and so I scold my little maid and enjoy good food hot from the kitchen and savour all the many different kinds of bread that we bake and enjoy ripe grapes and the juice from pomegranates. These things remain when others go. The children that I have loved most are now dead. Your father, Rē help him, was always a fool. I loved him when he was a toddling little boy, but now he irritates me with his airs of importance. Of my grandchildren I love you, Renisenb— and talking of grandchildren, where is Ipy? I have not seen him today or yesterday.'

'He is very busy superintending the storing of the grain. My father left him in charge.'

Esa grinned.

'That will please our young gander. He will be strutting about full of his own importance. When he comes in to eat tell him to come to me.'

'Yes, Esa.'

'For the rest, Renisenb, *silence* . . .'

*

'You wanted to see me, grandmother?'

Ipy stood smiling and arrogant, his head held a little on one side, a flower held between his white teeth. He looked very pleased with himself and with life generally.

'If you can spare a moment of your valuable time,' said Esa, screwing her eyes up to see better and looking him up and down.

The acerbity of her tone made no impression on Ipy.

'It is true that I am very busy today. I have to oversee everything since my father has gone to the Temple.'

'Young jackals bark loud,' said Esa.

But Ipy was quite imperturbable.

'Come, grandmother, you must have more to say to me than that.'

'Certainly I have more to say. And to begin with, this is a house of mourning. Your brother Sobek's body is already in the hands of the embalmers. Yet your face is as cheerful as though this was a festival day.'

Ipy grinned.

'You are no hypocrite, Esa. Would you have me be one? You know very well that there was no love lost between me and Sobek. He did everything he could to thwart and annoy me. He treated me as a child. He gave me all the most humiliating and childish tasks in the fields. Frequently he jeered and laughed at me. And when my father would have associated me with him in partnership, together with my elder brothers, it was Sobek who persuaded him not to do so.'

'What makes you think it was Sobek who persuaded him?' asked Esa sharply.

'Kameni told me so.'

'Kameni?' Esa raised her eyebrows, pushed her wig on one side and scratched her head. 'Kameni indeed. Now I find that interesting.'

'Kameni said he had it from Henet—and we all agree that Henet always knows everything.'

'Nevertheless,' said Esa drily, 'this is an occasion when Henet was wrong in her facts. Doubtless both Sobek and Yahmose were of opinion that you were too young for the business—but it was I—yes, I who dissuaded your father from including you.'

'You, grandmother? The boy stared at her in frank surprise. Then a dark scowl altered the expression of his face, the flower fell from his lips. 'Why should you do that? What business was it of yours?'

'My family's business is my business.'

'And my father listened to you?'

'Not at the moment,' said Esa drily. 'But I will teach you a lesson, my handsome child. Women work roundabout—and they learn (if they are not born with the knowledge) to play on the weaknesses of men. You may remember I sent Henet with the gaming board to the porch in the cool of the evening.'

'I remember. My father and I played together. What of it?'

'This. You played three games. And each time, being a much cleverer player, you beat your father.'

'Yes.'

'That is all,' said Esa, closing her eyes. 'Your father, like all inferior players, did not like being beaten—especially by a chit of a boy. So he remembered my words—and he decided that you were certainly too young to be given a share in the partnership.'

Ipy stared at her for a moment. Then he laughed—not a very pleasant laugh.

'You are clever, Esa,' he said. 'Yes, you may be old, but you are clever. Decidedly you and I have the brains of the family. You have pegged out in the first match on our gaming board. But you will see, I shall win the second. So look to yourself, grandmother.'

'I intend to,' said Esa. 'And in return for your words, let me advise *you* to look to *yourself*. One of your brothers is dead, the other has been near to death. You also are your father's son—and you may go the same way.'

Ipy laughed scornfully.

'There is little fear of that.'

'Why not? You also threatened and insulted Nofret.'

'Nofret!' Ipy's scorn was unmistakable.

'What is in your mind?' demanded Esa sharply.

'I have my ideas, grandmother. And I can assure you that Nofret and her spirit tricks will not worry me. Let her do her worst.'

There was a shrill wail behind him and Henet ran in crying out:

'Foolish boy—imprudent child. Defying the dead! And after we've all had a taste of her quality! And not so much as an amulet on you for protection!'

'Protection? I will protect myself. Get out of my way, Henet, I've got work to do. Those lazy peasants shall know what it is to have a real master over them.'

Pushing Henet aside, Ipy strode out of the room.

Esa cut short Henet's wails and lamentations.

'Listen to me, Henet, and stop exclaiming about Ipy. He may know what he is doing or he may not. His manner is very odd. But answer me this, did you tell Kameni that it was Sobek who had persuaded Imhotep not to include Ipy in the deed of association?'

Henet's voice dropped to its usual whining key.

'I'm sure I'm far too busy in the house to waste my time running about telling people things—and telling Kameni of all people. I'm sure I'd never speak a word to him if he didn't come and speak to me. He's got a pleasant manner, as you must admit yourself, Esa—and I'm not the only one who thinks so—oh dear no! And if a young widow wants to make a new contract, well, she usually fancies a handsome young man—though what Imhotep would say I'm sure I don't know. Kameni is only a junior scribe when all is said and done.'

'Never mind what Kameni is or isn't! Did you tell him that it was Sobek who opposed Ipy being made a partner in the association?'

'Well, really, Esa, I can't remember what I may or may not have said. I didn't actually go and tell anyone anything, that much is sure. But a word passed here and there, and you know yourself that Sobek was saying—and Yahmose too for that matter, though, of course, not so loud nor so often—that Ipy was a mere boy and that it would never do—and for all I know Kameni may have heard him say it himself and not got it from me at all. I never gossip—but after all, a tongue is given one to speak with and I'm not a deaf mute.'

'That you most certainly are not,' said Esa. 'A tongue,

Henet, may sometimes be a weapon. A tongue may cause a death—may cause more than one death. I hope *your* tongue, Henet, has not caused a death.'

'Why, Esa, the things you say! And what's in your mind? I'm sure I never say a word to anybody that I wouldn't be willing to let the whole world overhear. I'm so devoted to the whole family—I'd die for any one of them. Oh, they underestimate old Henet's devotion. I promised their dear mother—'

'Ha,' said Esa, cutting her short, 'here comes my plump reed bird, cooked with leeks and celery. It smells delicious—cooked to a turn. Since you're so devoted, Henet, you can take a little mouthful from one side—just in case it's poisoned.'

'Esa!' Henet gave a squeal. 'Poisoned! How can you say such things! And cooked in our very own kitchen.'

'Well,' said Esa, 'someone's got to taste it—just in case. And it had better be you, Henet, since you're so willing to die for any member of the family. I don't suppose it would be too painful a death. Come on, Henet. Look how plump and juicy and tasty it is. No, thanks, I don't want to lose my little slave girl. She's young and merry. You've passed your best days, Henet, and it wouldn't matter so much what happened to you. Now then—open your mouth . . . Delicious, isn't it? I declare—you're looking quite green in the face. Didn't you like my little joke? I don't believe you did. Ha ha, he he.'

Esa rolled about with merriment, then composing herself suddenly, she set greedily to work to eat her favourite dish.

CHAPTER 16

Second Month of Summer 1st Day

The consultation at the Temple was over. The exact form of the petition had been drawn up and amended. Hori and two Temple scribes had been busily employed. Now at last the first step had been taken.

The priest signed that the draft of the petition should be read out.

'To the Most Excellent Spirit Ashayet. This from your brother and husband. Has the sister forgotten her brother? Has the mother forgotten the children that were born to her? Does not the most excellent Ashayet know that a spirit of evil life menaces her children? Already is Sobek, her son, passed to Osiris by means of poison.

'I treated you in life with all honour. I gave you jewels and dresses, unguents and perfumes and oils for your limbs. Together we ate of good foods, sitting in peace and amity with tables loaded before us. When you were ill, I spared no expense. I procured for you a Master Physician. You were buried with all honour and

with due ceremonies and all things needful for your life in the hereafter were provided for you—servants and oxen and food and drink and jewels and raiment. I mourned for you many years—and after long long years only did I take a concubine so that I might live as befits a man not yet old.

'*This concubine it is that now does evil to your children. Do you not know of this? Perchance you are in ignorance. Surely if Ashayet knows, she will be swift to come to the aid of the sons born to her.*

'*Is it that Ashayet knows, but the evil is still done because the concubine is strong in evil magic? Yet surely it is against your will, most excellent Ashayet. Therefore reflect that in the Field of Offerings you have great relatives and powerful helpers. The great and noble Ipi, Chief Butler to the Visier. Invoke his aid! Also your mother's brother, the great and powerful Meriptah, the Nomarch of the Province. Acquaint him with the shameful truth. Let it be brought before his court. Let witnesses be summoned. Let them testify against Nofret that she has done this evil. Let judgement be given and may Nofret be condemned and let it be decreed that she do no more evil in this house.*

'*Oh, excellent Ashayet, if you are angry with this your brother Imhotep in that he did listen to this woman's evil persuasions and did threaten to do injustice to your children that were born of you, then reflect that it is not he alone that suffers, but your children also. Forgive your brother Imhotep aught that he has done for the sake of your children.*'

The Chief Scribe stopped reading. Mersu nodded approval.

'It is well expressed. Nothing, I think, has been left out.'

Imhotep rose.

'I thank you, Reverend Father. My offering shall reach you before tomorrow's sun sets—cattle, oil and flax. Shall we fix the day after that for the Ceremony—the placing of the inscribed bowl in the offering chamber of the Tomb?'

'Make it three days from now. The bowl must be inscribed and the preparations made for the necessary rites.'

'As you will. I am anxious that no more mischief should befall.'

'I can well understand your anxiety, Imhotep. But have no fear. The good spirit Ashayet will surely answer this appeal, and her kinsfolk have authority and power and can deal justice where it is so richly deserved.'

'May Isis allow that it be so! I thank you, Mersu—and for your care and cure of my son Yahmose. Come, Hori, we have much that must be seen to. Let us return to the house. Ah—this petition does indeed lift a weight off my mind. The excellent Ashayet will not fail her distracted brother.'

When Hori entered the courtyard, bearing his rolls of papyrus, Renisenb was watching for him. She came running from the lake.

'Hori!'

'Yes, Renisenb?'

'Will you come with me to Esa? She has been waiting and wants you.'

'Of course. Let me just see if Imhotep—'

But Imhotep had been buttonholed by Ipy and father and son were engaged in close conversation.

'Let me put down these scrolls and these other things and I will come with you, Renisenb.'

Esa looked pleased when Renisenb and Hori came to her.

'Here is Hori, grandmother. I brought him to you at once.'

'Good. Is the air pleasant outside?'

'I—I think so.' Renisenb was slightly taken aback.

'Then give me my stick. I will walk a little in the courtyard.'

Esa seldom left the house and Renisenb was surprised. She guided the old woman with a hand below her elbow. They went through the central hall and out on to the porch.

'Will you sit here, grandmother?'

'No, child, I will walk as far as the lake.'

Esa's progress was slow, but although she limped, she was strong on her feet and showed no signs of tiredness. Looking about her, she chose a spot where flowers had been planted in a little bed near the lake and where a sycamore fig tree gave welcome shade.

Then, once established, she said with grim satisfaction:

'There! Now we can talk and no one can overhear our talk.'

'You are wise, Esa,' said Hori approvingly.

'The things which have to be said must be known only to us three. I trust you, Hori. You have been with us since you were a little boy. You have always been faithful and discreet and wise. Renisenb here is the dearest to me of all my son's children. No harm must come to her, Hori.'

'No harm shall come to her, Esa.'

Hori did not raise his voice, but the tone of it and the look in his face as his eyes met the old woman's amply satisfied her.

'That is well said, Hori—quietly and without heat—but as one who means what he says. Now tell me what has been aranged today?'

Hori recounted the drawing up of the petition and the gist of it. Esa listened carefully.

'Now listen to me, Hori, and look at this.' She drew the lion necklace from her dress and handed it to him. She added: 'Tell him, Renisenb, where you found this.'

Renisenb did so. Then Esa said: 'Well, Hori, what do you think?'

Hori was silent for a moment, then he asked: 'You are old and wise, Esa. What do you think?'

Esa said: 'You are not of those, Hori, who do not like to speak rash words unaccompanied with facts. You knew, did you not, from the first how Nofret came to her death?'

'I suspected the truth, Esa. It was only suspicion.'

'Exactly. And we have only suspicion now. Yet here, by the lake, between us three, suspicion can be spoken—and afterwards not referred to again. Now it seems to me that there are three explanations of the tragic things that happened. The first is that the herd boy spoke the truth and that what he saw was indeed Nofret's ghost returned from the dead and that she had an evil determination to revenge herself still further by causing increased sorrow and grief to our family. That may be so—it is said by priests and others to be possible and we do know that illnesses are caused by evil spirits. But it seems to me, who am an old woman and who am not inclined to believe all that priests and others say, that there are other possibilities.'

'Such as?' asked Hori.

'Let us admit that Nofret was killed by Satipy, that some time afterwards at that same spot Satipy had a vision of Nofret and that, in her fear and guilt, she fell and died. That is all clear enough. But now let us come to another assumption; which is that after that someone, for a reason we have yet to discover, wished to cause the death of two of Imhotep's sons. That someone counted on a superstitious dread ascribing the deed to the spirit of Nofret—a singularly convenient assumption.'

'Who would want to kill Yahmose or Sobek?' cried Renisenb.

'Not a servant,' said Esa, 'they would not dare. That leaves us with but few people from whom to chose.'

'One of *ourselves*? But, grandmother, that could not be!'

'Ask Hori,' said Esa drily. 'You notice he makes no protest.'

Renisenb turned to him. 'Hori—surely—'

Hori shook his head gravely.

'Renisenb, you are young and trusting. You think that everyone you know and love is just as they appear to you. You do not know the human heart and the bitterness—yes, and evil—it may contain.'

'But who—which one—?'

Esa broke in briskly:

'Let us go back to this tale told by the herd boy. He saw a woman dressed in a dyed linen dress wearing Nofret's necklace. Now if it was no spirit, then he saw exactly what

170

he said he did—which means that he saw a woman who was deliberately trying to *appear* like Nofret. It might have been Kait—it might have been Henet—it might have been *you*, Renisenb! From that distance it might have been anyone wearing a woman's dress and a wig. Hush—let me go on. The other possibility is that the boy was lying. He told a tale that he had been *taught* to tell. He was obeying someone who had the right to command him and he may have been too dull-witted even to realize the point of the story he was bribed or cajoled to tell. We shall never know now because the boy is dead—in itself a suggestive point. It inclines me to the belief that the boy told a story he had been taught. Questioned closely, as he would have been today, that story could have been broken down—it is easy to discover with a little patience whether a child is lying.'

'So you think we have a poisoner in our midst?' asked Hori.

'I do,' said Esa. 'And you?'

'I think so too,' said Hori.

Renisenb glanced from one to the other of them in dismay.

Hori went on:

'But the motive seems to me far from clear.'

'I agree,' said Esa. 'That is why I am uneasy. *I do not know who is threatened next.*'

Renisenb broke in: 'But—one of *us*?' Her tone was still incredulous.

Esa said sternly: 'Yes, Renisenb—one of us. Henet or Kait or Ipy, or Kameni, or Imhotep himself—yes, or Esa or Hori or even—' she smiled—'Renisenb.'

'You are right, Esa,' said Hori. 'We must include ourselves.'

'But *why*?' Renisenb's voice held wondering horror. '*Why*?'

'If we knew that, we'd know very nearly all we wanted to know,' said Esa. 'We can only go by who was attacked. Sobek, remember, joined Yahmose unexpectedly after Yahmose had commenced to drink. Therefore it is *certain* that whoever did it wanted to kill Yahmose, less certain that that person wished also to kill Sobek.'

'But who could wish to kill Yahmose?' Renisenb spoke with sceptical intonation. 'Yahmose, surely, of us all would have no enemies. He is always quiet and kindly.'

'Therefore, clearly, the motive was not one of personal hate,' said Hori. 'As Renisenb says, Yahmose is not the kind of man who makes enemies.'

'No,' said Esa. 'The motive is more obscure than that. We have here either enmity against the family as a whole, or else there lies behind all these things that covetousness against which the Maxims of Ptahotep warn us. It is, he says, a bundle of every kind of evil and a bag of everything that is blameworthy!'

'I see the direction in which your mind is tending, Esa,' said Hori. 'But to arrive at any conclusion we shall have to make a forecast of the future.'

Esa nodded her head vigorously and her large wig slipped over one ear. Grotesque though this made her appearance, no one was inclined to laugh.

'Make such a forecast, Hori,' she said.

Hori was silent for a moment or two, his eyes thoughtful. The two women waited. Then, at last, he spoke.

'If Yahmose had died as intended, then the principal bene-
ficiaries would have been Imhotep's remaining sons, Sobek
and Ipy—some part of the estate would doubtless have been
set aside for Yahmose's children, but the administration of
it would have been in their hands—in Sobek's hands in
particular. Sobek would undoubtedly have been the greatest
gainer. He would presumably have functioned as ka-priest
during Imhotep's absences and would succeed to that office
after Imhotep's death. But though Sobek benefited, yet Sobek
cannot be the guilty person since he himself drank of the
poisoned wine so heartily that he died. Therefore, as far as
I can see, the deaths of these two can *benefit* only one person
(at the moment, that is) and that person is Ipy.'

'Agreed,' said Esa. 'But I note, Hori, that you are far-
seeing—and I appreciate your qualifying phrase. But let us
consider Ipy. He is young and impatient, he has in many
ways a bad disposition, he is at the age when the fulfilment
of what he desires seems to him the most important thing
in life. He felt anger and resentment against his elder
brothers and considered that he had been unjustly excluded
from participation in the family partnership. It seems, too,
that unwise things were said to him by Kameni—'

'Kameni?'

It was Renisenb who interrupted. Immediately she had
done so she flushed and bit her lip. Hori turned his head
to look at her. The long, gentle, penetrating look he gave
her hurt her in some indefinable way. Esa craned her neck
forward and peered at the girl.

'Yes,' she said. 'By Kameni. Whether or not inspired by
Henet is another matter. The fact remains that Ipy is

ambitious and arrogant, was resentful of his brothers' superior authority and that he definitely considers himself, as he told me long ago, the superior ruling intelligence of the family.'

Esa's tone was dry.

Hori asked: 'He said that to *you*?'

'He was kind enough to associate me with himself in the possession of a certain amount of intelligence.'

Renisenb demanded incredulously:

'You think Ipy deliberately poisoned Yahmose and Sobek?'

'I consider it a possibility, no more. This is suspicion that we talk now—we have not yet come to proof. Men have killed their brothers since the beginning of time, knowing that the Gods dislike such killing, yet driven by the evils of covetousness and hatred. And if Ipy did this thing, we shall not find it easy to get proof of what he did, for Ipy, I freely admit, is clever.'

Hori nodded.

'But as I say, it is suspicion we talk here, under the sycamore. And we will go on now to considering every member of the household in the light of suspicion. As I say, I exclude the servants because I do not believe for one moment that any one of them would dare do such a thing. But I do not exclude Henet.'

'Henet?' cried Renisenb. 'But Henet is devoted to us all. She never stops saying so.'

'It is as easy to utter lies as truth. I have known Henet for many years. I knew her when she came here as a young woman with your mother. She was a relative of hers—poor and unfortunate. Her husband had not cared for her—and indeed Henet was always plain and unattractive—and had divorced her. The one child she bore died in infancy. She came here professing herself devoted to your mother, but I have seen her eyes watching your mother as she moved about the house and courtyard—and I tell you, Renisenb, there was no love in them. No, sour envy was nearer the mark—and as to her professions of love for you all, I distrust them.'

'Tell me, Renisenb,' said Hori. 'Do you yourself feel affection towards Henet?'

'N-no,' said Renisenb unwillingly. 'I cannot. I have often reproached myself because I dislike her.'

'Don't you think that that is because, instinctively, you know her words are false? Does she ever show her reputed love for you by any real service? Has she not always fomented discord between you all by whispering and repeating things that are likely to wound and cause anger?'

'Yes—yes, that is true enough.'

Esa gave a dry chuckle.

'You have both eyes and ears in your head, most excellent Hori.'

Renisenb argued:

'But my father believes in her and is fond of her.'

'My son is a fool and always has been,' said Esa. 'All men like flattery—and Henet applies flattery as lavishly as unguents are applied at a banquet! She may be really devoted to him—sometimes I think she is—but certainly she is devoted to no one else in this house.'

'But surely she would not—she would not *kill*,' Renisenb protested. 'Why should she want to poison any of us? What good would it do her?'

'None. None. As to why—I know nothing of what goes on inside Henet's head. What she thinks, what she feels, that I do not know. But I sometimes think that strange things are brewing behind that cringing, fawning manner. And if so, her reasons are reasons that we, you and I and Hori, would not understand.'

Hori nodded. 'There is a rottenness that starts from within. I spoke to Renisenb once of that.'

'And I did not understand you,' said Renisenb. 'But I am beginning to understand better now. It began with the coming of Nofret—I saw then how none of us were quite what I had thought us to be. It made me afraid . . . And now—' she made a helpless gesture with her hands— 'everything is fear . . .'

'Fear is only incomplete knowledge,' said Hori. 'When we *know*, Renisenb, then there will be no more fear.'

'And then, of course, there is Kait,' proceeded Esa.

'Not Kait,' protested Renisenb. 'Kait would not try to kill Sobek. It is unbelievable.'

'Nothing is unbelievable,' said Esa. 'That at least I have learned in the course of my life. Kait is a thoroughly stupid woman and I have always mistrusted stupid women. They are dangerous. They can see only their own immediate surroundings and only one thing at a time. Kait lives at the core of a small world which is herself and her children and Sobek as her children's father. It might occur to her quite simply that to remove Yahmose would be to enrich her children. Sobek has always been unsatisfactory in Imhotep's eyes—he is rash, impatient of control and not amenable. Yahmose was the son on whom Imhotep relied. But with Yahmose gone, Imhotep would *have* to rely on Sobek. She would see it, I think, quite simply like that.'

Renisenb shivered. In spite of herself she recognized a true description of Kait's attitude to life. Her gentleness, her tenderness, her quiet loving ways were all directed to her own children. Outside herself and her children and Sobek, the world did not exist for her. She looked at it without curiosity and without interest.

Renisenb said slowly: 'But surely she would have realized that it was quite possible for Sobek to come back, as he did, thirsty and also drink the wine?'

'No,' said Esa. 'I don't think that she would. Kait, as I say, is stupid. She would see only what she wanted to see—Yahmose drinking and dying and the business being put down to the magical intervention of our evil and beautiful Nofret. She would see only one simple thing—not various possibilities or probabilities, and since she did not want Sobek to die, it would never occur to her that he might come back unexpectedly.'

'And now Sobek is dead and Yahmose is living! How terrible that must be for her if what you suggest is true.'

'It is the kind of thing that happens to you when you are stupid,' said Esa. 'Things go entirely differently from the way you planned them.'

She paused and then went on:

'And now we come to Kameni.'

'Kameni?' Renisenb felt it necessary to say the word

quietly and without protest. Once again she was uncomfortably aware of Hori's eyes on her.

'Yes, we cannot exclude Kameni. He has no known motive for injuring us—but then what do we really know of him? He comes from the North—from the same part of Egypt as Nofret. He helped her, willingly or unwillingly, who can say?—to turn Imhotep's heart against the children that had been born to him. I have watched him sometimes and in truth I can make little of him. He seems to me, on the whole, a commonplace young man with a certain shrewdness of mind, and also, besides being handsome, with a certain something that draws after him the eyes of women. Yes, women will always like Kameni and yet I think—I may be wrong—that he is not one of those who have a real hold on their hearts and minds. He seems always gay and lighthearted and he showed no great concern at the time of Nofret's death.

'But all this is outward seeming. Who can tell what goes on in the human heart? A determined man could easily play a part . . . Does Kameni in reality passionately resent Nofret's death, and does he seek to exact revenge for it? Since Satipy killed Nofret, must Yahmose, her husband, also die? Yes, and Sobek too, who threatened her—and perhaps Kait who persecuted her in petty ways, and Ipy who also hated her? It seems fantastic, but who can tell?'

Esa paused. She looked at Hori.

'Who can tell, Esa?'

Esa peered at him shrewdly.

'Perhaps you can tell, Hori? You think you know, do you not?'

Hori was silent for a moment, then he said:

'I have an idea of my own, yes, as to who poisoned that wine and why—but it is not as yet very clear—and indeed I do not see—' He paused for a minute, frowning, then shook his head. 'No, I could make no definite accusation.'

'We talk only suspicion here. Go on, Hori, speak.'

Hori shook his head.

'No, Esa. It is only a nebulous thought . . . And if it were true then it is better for you not to know. The knowledge might be dangerous. And the same applies to Renisenb.'

'Then the knowledge is dangerous to you, Hori?'

'Yes, it is dangerous . . . I think, Esa, that we are all in danger—though Renisenb, perhaps, least.'

Esa looked at him for some time without speaking.

'I would give a great deal,' she said at last, 'to know what is in your mind.'

Hori did not reply directly. He said, after a moment or two during which he seemed to be thinking:

'The only clue to what is in people's minds is in their behaviour. If a man behaves strangely, oddly, is not himself—'

'Then you suspect him?' asked Renisenb.

'No,' said Hori. 'That is just what I mean. A man whose mind is evil and whose intentions are evil is conscious of that fact and he knows that he must conceal it at all costs. He dare not, therefore, afford any unusual behaviour . . .'

'A man?' asked Esa.

'Man or woman—it is the same.'

'I see,' said Esa. She threw him a very sharp glance. Then

she said: 'And what of us? What of suspicion where we three are concerned?'

'That, too, must be faced,' said Hori. 'I have been much trusted. The making of contracts and the disposal of crops has been in my hands. As scribe I have dealt with all the accounts. It could be that I had falsified them—as Kameni discovered had been done in the North. Then Yahmose, it may be, might have been puzzled, he might have begun to suspect. Therefore it would be necessary for me to silence Yahmose.' He smiled faintly at his own words.

'Oh, Hori,' said Renisenb, 'how can you say such things! No one who knew you would believe them.'

'No one, Renisenb, knows anyone else. Let me tell you that yet once more.'

'And I?' said Esa. 'Where does suspicion point in my case? Well, I am old. When a brain grows old, it turns sick sometimes. It hates where it used to love. I may be weary of my children's children and seek to destroy my own blood. It is an affliction of an evil spirit that happens sometimes to those who are old.'

'And I?' asked Renisenb. 'Why should I try to kill my brothers whom I love?'

Hori said:

'If Yahmose and Sobek and Ipy were dead, then you would be the last of Imhotep's children. He would find you a husband and all here would come to you—and you and your husband would be guardians to Yahmose's and Sobek's children.'

Then he smiled.

180

'But under the sycamore tree, we do not suspect you, Renisenb.'

'Under the sycamore tree, or not under the sycamore tree, we love you,' said Esa.

CHAPTER 17

Second Month of Summer 1st Day

'So you have been outside the house?' said Henet, bustling in as Esa limped into the room. 'A thing you have not done for almost a year!'

Her eyes looked inquisitively at Esa.

'Old people,' said Esa, 'have whims.'

'I saw you sitting by the lake—with Hori and Renisenb.'

'Pleasant company, both of them. Is there ever anything you do *not* see, Henet?'

'Really, Esa, I don't know what you mean! You were sitting there plain enough for all the world to see.'

'But not near enough for all the world to hear!'

Esa grinned and Henet bridled angrily.

'I don't know why you're so unkind to me, Esa! You're always suggesting things. I'm much too busy seeing that things are done as they should be in this house to listen to other people's conversations. What do *I* care what people say!'

'I've often wondered.'

'If it were not for Imhotep who *does* appreciate me—'

Esa cut in sharply:

'Yes, if it were not for Imhotep! It is on Imhotep you depend, is it not? If anything were to happen to Imhotep—'

It was Henet's turn to interrupt.

'Nothing will happen to Imhotep!'

'How do you know, Henet? Is there such safety in this house? Something has happened to Yahmose and Sobek.'

'That is true—Sobek died—and Yahmose nearly died—'

'Henet!' Esa leaned forward. '*Why did you smile when you said that?*'

'I? Smile?' Henet was taken aback. 'You are dreaming, Esa! Is it likely I should smile—at such a moment—talking of such a terrible thing!'

'It is true that I am nearly blind,' said Esa. 'But I am not quite blind. Sometimes, by a trick of light, by a screwing up of the eyelids, I see very well. It can happen that if anyone is talking to a person they know cannot see well, they are careless. They permit themselves an expression of face that on other occasions they would not allow. So I ask you again: Why do you smile with such secret satisfaction?'

'What you say is outrageous—quite outrageous!'

'Now you are frightened.'

'And who would not be with the things going on in this house?' cried Henet shrilly. 'We're all afraid, I'm sure, with evil spirits returning from the dead to torment us! But I know what it is, you've been listening to Hori. What did he say about me?'

'What does Hori know about you, Henet?'

'Nothing—nothing at all. You'd better ask what do *I* know about *him*?'

Agatha Christie

Esa's eyes grew sharp.

'Well, what do you know?'

Henet tossed her head.

'Ah, you all despise poor Henet! You think she's ugly and stupid. But I know what's going on! There are a lot of things I know—indeed there's not much I *don't* know of what goes on in this house. I may be stupid, but I can count how many beans are planted to a row. Maybe I see more than clever people like Hori do. When Hori meets me anywhere he has a trick of looking as though I didn't exist, as though he saw something behind me, something that isn't there. He'd better look *at* me, that's what I say! He may think me negligible and stupid—but it's not always the clever ones who know everything. Satipy thought she was clever, and where is she now, I should like to know?'

Henet paused triumphantly—then a qualm seemed to pass over her, and she visibly cringed a little, glancing nervously at Esa.

But Esa seemed lost in some train of thought of her own. She had a shocked, almost frightened look of bewilderment on her face. She said slowly and musingly:

'Satipy . . .'

Henet said in her old whining tone:

'I'm sorry, Esa, I'm sure, for losing my temper. Really, I don't know what came over me. I didn't mean anything of what I've been saying . . .'

Looking up, Esa cut her short.

'Go away, Henet. Whether you meant what you said, or did not mean what you said does not really matter. But

184

you have uttered one phrase which has awakened new
thoughts in my mind . . . Go, Henet, and I warn you—Be
careful of your words and actions. *We want no more deaths
in this house.* I hope you understand.'

Everything is fear . . .

Renisenb had found those words rising to her lips auto-
matically during the consultation by the lake. It was only
afterwards that she began to realize their truth.

She set out mechanically to join Kait and the children
where they were clustered by the little pavilion, but found
that her footsteps lagged and then ceased as if of their own
volition.

She was afraid, she found, to join Kait, to look into that
plain and placid face, in case she might fancy she saw there
the face of a poisoner. She watched Henet bustle out on
the porch and back again and her usual sense of repulsion
was, she found, heightened. Desperately she turned towards
the doorway of the courtyard, and a moment later encoun-
tered Ipy striding in, his head held high and a gay smile
on his impudent face.

Renisenb found herself staring at him. Ipy, the spoilt
child of the family, the handsome, wilful little boy she
remembered when she had gone away with Khay . . .

'Why, Renisenb, what is it? Why are you looking at me
so strangely?'

'Was I?'

Ipy laughed.

'You are looking as half-witted as Henet.'

Renisenb shook her head.

'Henet is not half-witted. She is very astute.'

'She has plenty of malice, that I know. In fact she's a nuisance about the house. I mean to get rid of her.'

Renisenb's lips opened and closed. She whispered, 'Get rid of her?'

'My dear sister, what is the matter with you? Have you, too, been seeing evil spirits like that miserable, half-witted black child?'

'You think everyone is half-witted!'

'That child certainly was. Well, it's true I'm inclined to be impatient of stupidity. I've had too much of it. It's no fun, I can tell you, being plagued with two slow-going elder brothers who can't see beyond their own noses! Now that they are out of the way, and there is only my father to deal with, you will soon see the difference. My father will do what *I* say.'

Renisenb looked up at him. He looked unusually handsome and arrogant. There was a vitality about him, a sense of triumphant life and vigour, that struck her as above the normal. Some inner consciousness seemed to be affording him this vital sense of well-being.

Renisenb said sharply:

'My brothers are not both out of the way, as you put it. Yahmose is alive.'

Ipy looked at her with an air of contemptuous mockery.

'And I suppose you think he will get quite well again?'

'Why not?'

Ipy laughed.

'Why not? Well, let us say simply that I disagree with you. Yahmose is finished, done for—he may crawl about

186

for a little and sit and moan in the sun. But he is no longer a man. He has recovered from the first effects of the poison, but you can see, yourself, he makes no further headway.'

'Then why doesn't he?' Renisenb demanded. 'The physician said it would only take a little time before he was quite strong and himself again.'

Ipy shrugged his shoulders.

'Physicians do not know everything. They talk wisely and use long words. Blame the wicked Nofret if you like— but Yahmose, your dear brother Yahmose, is doomed.'

'And have you no fear yourself, Ipy?'

'Fear? I?' The boy laughed, throwing back his handsome head.

'Nofret did not love you overwell, Ipy.'

'Nothing can harm me, Renisenb, unless I choose to let it! I am young still, but I am one of those people who are born to succeed. As for you, Renisenb, you would do well to be on my side, do you hear? You treat me, often, as an irresponsible boy. But I am more than that now. Every month will show a difference. Soon there will be no will but mine in this place. My father may give the orders, but though his voice speaks them, the brain that conceives them will be mine!' He took a step or two, paused, and said over his shoulder: 'So be careful, Renisenb, that I do not become displeased with *you*.'

As Renisenb stood staring after him, she heard a footstep and turned to see Kait standing beside her.

'What was Ipy saying, Renisenb?'

Renisenb said slowly:

'He says that he will be master here soon.'
'Does he?' said Kait. 'I think otherwise.'

Ipy ran lightly up the steps of the porch and into the house.

The sight of Yahmose lying on a couch seemed to please him. He said gaily:

'Well, how goes it, brother? Are we never to see you back on the cultivation? I cannot understand why everything has not gone to pieces without you!'

Yahmose said fretfully in a weak voice:

'I do not understand it at all. The poison is now eliminated. Why do I not regain my strength? I tried to walk this morning and my legs would not support me. I am weak—weak—and what is worse, I seem to grow weaker every day.'

Ipy shook his head with facile commiseration.

'That is indeed bad. And the physicians give no help?'

'Mersu's assistant comes every day. He cannot understand my condition. I drink strong decoctions of herbs. The daily incantations are made to the goddess. Special food full of nourishment is prepared for me. There is no reason, so the physician assures me, why I should not rapidly grow strong. Yet instead, I seem to waste away.'

'That is too bad,' said Ipy.

He went on, singing softly under his breath till he came upon his father and Hori engaged with a sheet of accounts.

Imhotep's face, anxious and careworn, lightened at the sight of his much-loved youngest son.

'Here is my Ipy. What have you to report from the estate?'

'All goes well, father. We have been reaping the barley. A good crop.'

'Yes, thanks to Rē all goes well outside. Would it went as well inside. Still I must have faith in Ashayet—she will not refuse to aid us in our distress. I am worried about Yahmose. I cannot understand this lassitude—the unaccountable weakness.'

Ipy smiled scornfully.

'Yahmose was always a weakling,' he said.

'That is not so,' said Hori mildly. 'His health has always been good.'

Ipy said assertively:

'Health depends on the spirit of a man. Yahmose never had any spirit. He was afraid, even, to give orders.'

'That is not so lately,' said Imhotep. 'Yahmose has shown himself to be full of authority in these last months. I have been surprised. But this weakness in the limbs worries me. Mersu assured me that once the effects of the poison had worn off, recovery should be swift.'

Hori moved some of the papyrus aside.

'There are other poisons,' he said quietly.

'What do you mean?' Imhotep wheeled round.

Hori spoke in a gentle, speculative voice.

'There are poisons known which do not act at once, with violence. They are insidious. A little taken every day accumulates in the system. Only after long months of weakness, does death come . . . There is a knowledge of such things among women—they use them sometimes to remove a husband and to make it seem as though his death were natural.'

Imhotep grew pale.

'Do you suggest that that—*that*—is what is the matter with Yahmose?'

'I am suggesting that it is a possibility. Though his food is now tasted by a slave before he gets it, such a precaution means nothing, since the amount in any one dish on any one day would cause no ill effect.'

'Folly,' cried Ipy, loudly. 'Absolute folly! I do not believe there are such poisons. *I* have never heard of them.'

Hori raised his eyes. 'You are very young, Ipy. There are still things you do not know.'

Imhotep exclaimed, 'But what can we do? We have appealed to Ashayet. We have sent offerings to the Temple—not that I have ever had much belief in temples. It is women who are credulous about such things. What more can be done?'

Hori said thoughtfully:

'Let Yahmose's food be prepared by one trustworthy slave, and let that slave be watched all the time.'

'But that means—that *here* in this house—'

'Rubbish,' shouted Ipy. 'Absolute rubbish.'

Hori raised his eyebrows.

'Let it be tried,' he said. 'We shall soon see if it is rubbish.'

Ipy went angrily out of the room. Hori stared thoughtfully after him with a perplexed frown on his face.

Ipy went out of the house in such a rage that he almost knocked over Henet.

'Get out of my way, Henet. You are always creeping about and getting in the way.'

'How rough you are, Ipy, you have bruised my arm.'

'A good thing. I am tired of you and your snivelling ways. The sooner you are out of this house for good the better—and I shall see that you go.'

Henet's eyes flashed maliciously.

'So you would turn me out, would you? After all the care and love I have bestowed on you all. Devoted, I've been, to the whole family. Your father knows it well enough.'

'He's heard about it enough, I'm sure! And so have we! In my opinion you're just an evil-tongued old mischief maker. You helped Nofret with her schemes—that I know well enough. Then she died and you came fawning round us again. But you'll see—in the end my father will listen to *me* and not to your lying tales.'

'You're very angry, Ipy, what has made you angry?'

'Never mind.'

'You're not afraid of something are you, Ipy? There are odd things going on here.'

'You can't frighten me, you old cat.'

He flung himself past her and out of the house.

Henet turned slowly inwards. A groan from Yahmose attracted her attention. He had raised himself from the couch and was trying to walk. But his legs seemed to fail him almost at once, and but for Henet's rapid assistance he would have fallen to the ground.

'There, Yahmose, there. Lie back again.'

'How strong you are, Henet. One would not think it to look at you.' He settled back again with his head on the wooden headrest. 'Thank you. But what is the matter with me? Why this feeling as though my muscles were turned into water?'

'The matter is that this house is bewitched. The work of a she-devil who came to us from the North. No good ever came out of the North.'

Yahmose murmured with sudden despondency:

'I am dying. Yes, I am dying . . .'

'Others will die before you,' said Henet, grimly.

'What? What do you mean?' He raised himself on an elbow and stared at her.

'I know what I am saying.' Henet nodded her head several times. 'It is not you who will die next. Wait and see.'

'Why do you avoid me, Renisenb?'

Kameni planted himself directly in Renisenb's way. She flushed and found it difficult to give a suitable answer. It was true that she had deliberately turned aside when she saw Kameni coming.

'Why, Renisenb, tell me why?'

But she had no answer ready, could only shake her head dumbly.

Then she glanced up at him as he stood facing her. She had had a faint dread that Kameni's face, too, might seem different. It was with a curious gladness that she saw it unchanged, his eyes looked at her gravely and there was for once no smile upon his lips.

Before the look in his eyes her own fell. Kameni could always disturb her. His nearness affected her physically. Her heart beat a shade faster.

'I know why you avoid me, Renisenb.'

She found her voice.

'I—was not avoiding you. I did not see you coming.'

'That is a lie.' He was smiling now, she could hear it in his voice.

'Renisenb, beautiful Renisenb.'

She felt his warm, strong hand around her arm and immediately she shook herself free.

'Do not touch me! I do not like to be touched.'

'Why do you fight against me, Renisenb? You know well enough the thing that is between us. You are young and strong and beautiful. It is against nature that you should go on grieving for a husband all your life. I will take you away from this house. It is full of deaths and evil spells. You shall come away with me and be safe.'

'And suppose I do not want to come?' said Renisenb with spirit.

Kameni laughed. His teeth gleamed white and strong.

'But you do want to come, only you will not admit it! Life is good, Renisenb, when a sister and brother are together. I will love you and make you happy and you shall be a glorious field to me, your Lord. See, I shall no longer sing to Ptah, "*Give me my sister tonight*," but I shall go to Imhotep and say, "Give me my sister Renisenb." But I think it is not safe for you here, so I shall take you away. I am a good scribe and I can enter the household of one of the great nobles of Thebes if I wish, though

actually I like the country life here—the cultivation and
the cattle and the songs of the men who reap, and the
little pleasure craft on the river. I would like to sail with
you on the river, Renisenb. And we will take Teti with
us. She is a beautiful, strong child and I will love her
and be a good father to her. Come, Renisenb, what do
you say?'

Renisenb stood silent. She was conscious of her heart
beating fast and she felt a kind of languor stealing over
her senses. Yet with this feeling of softness, this yielding,
went something else—a feeling of antagonism.

'The touch of his hand on my arm and I am all weakness . . .' she thought. 'Because of his strength . . . of
his square shoulders . . . his laughing mouth . . . But I
know nothing of his mind, of his thoughts, of his heart.
There is no peace between us and no sweetness . . . What
do I want? I do not know . . . But not this . . . No, not
this—'

She heard herself saying, and even in her own ears the
words sounded weak and uncertain:

'I do not want another husband . . . I want to be
alone . . . to be myself . . .'

'No, Renisenb, you are wrong. You were not meant to
live alone. Your hand says so when it trembles with
mine . . . See?'

With an effort Renisenb drew her hand away.

'I do not love you, Kameni. I think I hate you.'

He smiled.

'I do not mind your hating me, Renisenb. Your hate is
very close to love. We will speak of this again.'

He left her, moving with the swiftness and easy gait of a young gazelle. Renisenb went slowly on to where Kait and the children were playing by the lake.

Kait spoke to her, but Renisenb answered at random.

Kait, however, did not seem to notice, or else, as usual, her mind was too full of the children to pay much attention to other things.

Suddenly, breaking the silence, Renisenb said:

'Shall I take another husband? What do you say, Kait?'

Kait replied placidly without any great interest:

'It would be as well, I think. You are strong and young, Renisenb, and you can have many more children.'

'Is that all a woman's life, Kait? To busy myself in the back of the house, to have children, to spend the afternoons with them by the lake under the sycamore trees?'

'It is all that matters to a woman. Surely you know that. Do not speak as though you were a slave—women have power in Egypt—inheritance passes through them to their children. Women are the life blood of Egypt.'

Renisenb looked thoughtfully at Teti who was busily making a garland of flowers for her doll. Teti was frowning a little with the concentration of what she was doing. There had been a time when Teti had looked so like Khay, pushing out her underlip, turning her head a little sideways, that Renisenb's heart had turned over with pain and love. But now not only was Khay's face dim in Renisenb's memory, but Teti no longer had that trick of head turning and pushing out her lip. There had been other moments when Renisenb had held Teti close to her, feeling the child still part of her own body, her own living flesh, with a

195

passionate sense of ownership. 'She is mine, all mine,' she had said to herself.

Now watching her, Renisenb thought, 'She is *me*—and she is *Khay*—'

Then Teti looked up, and seeing her mother, she smiled. It was a grave, friendly smile, with confidence in it and pleasure.

Renisenb thought: 'No, she is not me and she is not Khay—she is *herself*. She is Teti. She is alone, as I am alone, as we are all alone. If there is love between us we shall be friends all our life—but if there is not love she will grow up and we shall be strangers. She is Teti and I am Renisenb.'

Kait was looking at her curiously.

'What *do* you want, Renisenb? I do not understand.'

Renisenb did not answer. How put into words for Kait the things she hardly understood herself. She looked round her, at the courtyard walls, at the gaily coloured porch of the house, at the smooth waters of the lake and the graceful little pleasure pavilion, the neat flower beds and the clumps of papyrus. All safe, shut in, nothing to fear, with around her the murmur of the familiar home sounds, the babble of children's voices, the raucous, far-off shrill clamour of women in the house, the distant lowing of cattle.

She said slowly:

'One cannot see the river from here . . .'

Kait looked surprised. 'Why should one want to see it?'

Renisenb said slowly:

'I am stupid. I do not know . . .'

Before her eyes, very clearly, she saw spread out the panorama of green fields, rich and lush, and beyond, far away, an enchanted distance of pale rose and amethyst fading into the horizon, and cleaving the two, the pale silver blue of the Nile . . .

She caught her breath—for with the vision, the sights and sounds around her faded—there came instead a stillness, a richness, an infinite satisfaction . . .

She said to herself: 'If I turn my head, I shall see Hori. He will look up from his papyrus and smile at me . . . Presently the sun will set and there will be darkness and then I shall sleep . . . That will be death.'

'What did you say, Renisenb?'

Renisenb started. She was not aware she had spoken aloud. She came back from her vision to reality. Kait was looking at her curiously.

'You said "*Death*", Renisenb. What were you thinking?'

Renisenb shook her head.

'I don't know. I didn't mean—' She looked round her again. How pleasant it was, this family scene, with the splashing water, and the children at play. She drew a deep breath.

'How peaceful it is here. One can't imagine anything— horrible—happening here.'

But it was by the lake that they found Ipy the next morning. He was sprawled face downwards with his face in the water where a hand had held him while he drowned.

CHAPTER 18

Second Month of Summer 10th Day

Imhotep sat huddled down upon himself. He looked very much older, a broken shrunken old man. On his face was a piteous look of bewilderment.

Henet brought him food and coaxed him to take it.

'Yes, yes, Imhotep, you must keep up your strength.'

'Why should I? What is strength? Ipy was strong—strong in youth and beauty—and now he lies in the brine bath . . . My son, my dearly loved son. The last of my sons.'

'No, no, Imhotep—you have Yahmose, your good Yahmose.'

'For how long? No, he too is doomed. We are all doomed. What evil is this that has come upon us? Could I know that such things would come of taking a concubine into my house? It is an accepted thing to do—it is righteous and according to the law of men and Gods. I treated her with honour. Why, then, should these things come upon me? Or is it Ashayet who wreaks vengeance upon me? Is it she who will not forgive? Certainly she has made no answer to my petition. The evil business still goes on.'

'No, no, Imhotep. You must not say that. So short a time has passed since the bowl was placed in the offering chamber. Does one not know how long affairs of law and justice take in this world—how endless are the delays in the Nomarch's court—and still more when a case goes up to the Vizier. Justice is justice, in this world and the next, a business that moves slowly but is adjusted with righteousness in the end.'

Imhotep shook his head doubtfully. Henet went on.

'Besides, Imhotep, you must remember that Ipy was not Ashayet's son—he was born to your sister Ankh. Why, then, should Ashayet concern herself violently on his behalf? But with Yahmose, it will be different—Yahmose will recover because Ashayet will see to it that he does.'

'I must admit, Henet, that your words comfort me . . . There is much in what you say. Yahmose, it is true, recovers strength now every day. He is a good loyal son—but oh! for my Ipy—such spirit—such beauty!' Imhotep groaned anew.

'Alas! Alas!' Henet wailed in sympathy.

'That accursed girl and her beauty! Would I had never set eyes on her.'

'Yes, indeed, dear master. A daughter of Seth if ever I saw one. Learned in magic and evil spells, there can be no doubt about it.'

There was a tap of a stick on the floor and Esa came limping into the hall. She gave a derisive snort.

'Has no one in this house any sense? Have you nothing better to do than bleat out curses against an unfortunate girl who took your fancy and who indulged in a little feminine spite and malice, goaded by the stupid behaviour of the stupid wives of your stupid sons?'

'A little spiteful malice—is that what you call it, Esa? When, of my three sons, two are dead and one is dying! Oh! that my mother should say such things to me!'

'It seems necessary that someone should say them since you cannot recognize facts for what they are. Wipe out of your mind this silly superstitious belief that a dead girl's spirit is working this evil. It was a *live* hand that held Ipy head down in the lake to drown, and a live hand that dropped poison into the wine that Yahmose and Sobek drank. You have an enemy, yes, Imhotep, but an enemy here in this house. And the proof is that since Hori's advice was taken and Renisenb herself prepares Yahmose's food, or a slave prepares it while she watches and that her hand carries it to him, since then, I say, Yahmose has gained health and strength every day. Try to stop being a fool, Imhotep, and moaning and beating your head—in all of which Henet is being extremely helpful—'

'Oh, Esa, how you misjudge me!'

'In which, I say, Henet assists you—either because she is a fool too, or for some other reason—'

'May Rē forgive you, Esa, for your unkindness to a poor lonely woman!'

Esa swept on, shaking her stick in an impressive gesture.

'Pull yourself together, Imhotep, and *think*. Your dead wife Ashayet, who was a very lovely woman and *not* a fool, by the way, may exert her influence for you in the other world, but can hardly be expected to do your thinking for you in this one! We have got to *act*, for if we do not then there will be more deaths.'

'A live enemy? An enemy in this house? You really believe that, Esa?'

'Of course I believe it, because it is the only thing that makes sense.'

'But then we are all in danger?'

'Certainly we are. In danger not of spells and spirit hands, but of human agency—of live fingers that drop poison in food and drink, of a human figure that steals up behind a boy who returns late at night from the village and forces his head down into the waters of the lake!'

Imhotep said thoughtfully: 'Strength would be needed for that.'

'On the face of it, yes, but I am not sure. Ipy had drunk much beer in the village. He was in a wild and boastful mood. It may be that he returned home unsteady on his feet and that, having no fear of the person who accosted him, he bent of his own accord to bathe his face in the lake. Little strength would be needed then.'

'What are you trying to say, Esa? That a *woman* did this thing? But it is impossible—the whole thing is impossible—there can be no enemy in this house or we should know it—*I* should know it!'

'There is an evil of the heart, Imhotep, that does not show in the face.'

'You mean that one of our servants, or a slave—'

'No servant and no slave, Imhotep.'

'One of ourselves? Or else—do you mean Hori or Kameni? But Hori is one of the family, he has proved himself faithful and trustworthy. And Kameni—he is a stranger, true, but he is of our blood and he has proved his devotion by his zeal in my service. Moreover he came to me only this morning and urged that I should consent to his marriage with Renisenb.'

'Oh, he did, did he?' Esa showed interest. 'And what did you say?'

'What could I say?' Imhotep was fretful. 'Is this a time to talk of marriage? I said as much to him.'

'And what did he say to that?'

'He said that in his opinion this *was* the time to talk of marriage. He said that Renisenb was not safe in this house.'

'I wonder,' said Esa. 'I very much wonder . . . Is she? I thought she was—and Hori thought so—but now . . .'

Imhotep went on.

'Can one have marriages and funeral ceremonies going on side by side? It is not decent. The whole Nome would talk about it.'

'This is no time for convention,' said Esa. 'Especially since it would seem that the embalmers' men are with us permanently. All this must be a blessing to Ipi and Montu—the firm must be doing exceptionally well.'

'They have put their charges up by ten per cent!' Imhotep was momentarily diverted. 'Iniquitous! They say that labour is more expensive.'

'They should give us a cut rate price for quantity!' Esa smiled grimly at her joke.

'My dear mother,' Imhotep looked at her in horror. 'This is not a jest.'

'All life is a jest, Imhotep—and it is death who laughs last.

Do you not hear it at every feast? Eat, drink and be merry for tomorrow you die? Well, that is very true for us here—it is a question only of *whose* death will come tomorrow.'

'What you say is terrible—terrible! What can be done?'

'Trust no one,' said Esa. 'That is the first, the most vital thing.' She repeated with emphasis: '*Trust no one.*'

Henet began to sob.

'Why do you look at *me* . . . I'm sure if anyone is worthy of trust, I am. I've proved it over all these years. Don't listen to her, Imhotep.'

'There, there, my good Henet—naturally I trust you. I know only too well your true and devoted heart.'

'You know nothing,' said Esa. 'None of us know anything. That is our danger.'

'You accused *me*,' whined Henet.

'I cannot accuse. I have neither knowledge nor proof—only suspicion.'

Imhotep looked up sharply.

'You have suspicion—of whom?'

Esa said slowly: 'I have suspected once—and twice—and a third time. I will be honest, I suspected first Ipy—but Ipy is dead, so that suspicion was false. Then I suspected another person—but, on the very day of Ipy's death, yet a third idea came to me . . .'

She paused.

'Are Hori and Kameni in the house? Send for them here—yes, and Renisenb too from the kitchen. And Kait and Yahmose. I have something to say and all the house should hear it.'

*

Agatha Christie

Esa looked round at the assembled family. She met Yahmose's grave and gentle glance, Kameni's ready smile, the frightened inquiry in Renisenb's eyes, the placid incurious glance of Kait, the quiet inscrutability of Hori's thoughtful gaze, the irritable fear of Imhotep's twitching face and the avid curiosity and—yes—pleasure in Henet's eyes.

She thought: 'Their faces tell me nothing. They show only the outward emotion. Yet surely, if I am right, there must be *some* betrayal.'

Aloud she said: 'I have something to say to you all—but first I will speak only to Henet—here in front of all of you.'

Henet's expression changed—the avidity and the pleasure went out of it. She looked frightened. Her voice rose in a shrill protest.

'You suspect me, Esa. I knew it! You will make a case against me and how am I, a poor woman with no great wits, to defend myself? I shall be condemned—condemned unheard.'

'Not unheard,' said Esa with irony and saw Hori smile.

Henet went on, her voice growing more and more hysterical.

'I have done nothing—I am innocent . . . Imhotep, my dearest master, save me . . .' She flung herself down and clasped him round the knees. Imhotep began to splutter indignantly, meanwhile patting Henet's head.

'Really, Esa, I protest—this is disgraceful . . .'

Esa cut him short.

'I have made no accusation—I do not accuse without

proof. I ask only that Henet shall explain to us here the meaning of certain things she has said.'

'I have said nothing—nothing at all . . .'

'Oh yes, you have,' said Esa. 'There are words I heard with my own ears—and my ears are sharp even if my eyes are dim. You said that you knew something about Hori. Now what is it that you know about Hori?'

Hori looked slightly surprised.

'Yes, Henet,' he said. 'What do you know about me? Let us have it.'

Henet sat back on her haunches and wiped her eyes. She looked sullen and defiant.

'I know nothing,' she said. 'What should I know?'

'That is what we are waiting for you to tell us,' said Hori.

Henet shrugged her shoulders.

'I was just talking. I meant nothing.'

Esa said: 'I will repeat to you your own words. You said that we all despised you, but that you knew a lot of what was going on in this house—and that you saw more than many clever people saw.

'And then you said this—that when Hori met you, he looked at you as though you didn't exist, as though he saw something behind you—*something that wasn't there.*'

'He always looks like that,' said Henet sullenly. 'I might be an insect, the way he looks at me—something that practically doesn't matter.'

Esa said slowly:

'That phrase has remained in my mind—something behind—*something that wasn't there.* Henet said, "He should have looked at *me*." And she went on to speak of Satipy—yes, of Satipy—and of how Satipy was clever, but where was Satipy now? . . .'

Esa looked round.

'Does that mean nothing to any of you? Think of Satipy—Satipy who is dead . . . And remember one should look *at* a person—not at something that isn't there . . .'

There was a moment's dead silence and then Henet screamed. It was a high, thin scream—a scream, it would seem, of sheer terror. She cried out incoherently:

'I didn't—save me—master, don't let her . . . I've said nothing—nothing.'

Imhotep's pent up rage burst out.

'This is unpardonable,' he roared. 'I will not have this poor woman terrified and accused. What have you against her? By your own words, nothing at all.'

Yahmose joined in without his usual timidity.

'My father is right. If you have a definite accusation to bring against Henet, bring it.'

'I do not accuse her,' said Esa slowly.

She leaned on her stick. Her figure seemed to have shrunk. She spoke slowly and heavily.

Yahmose turned with authority to Henet.

'Esa is not accusing you of causing the evils that have happened, but if I understand her rightly, she thinks that you have certain knowledge which you are withholding. Therefore, Henet, if there is anything you know, about Hori or another, now is the time to speak. Here, before us all. Speak. What knowledge have you?'

Henet shook her head.

'None.'

'Be very sure of what you are saying, Henet. Knowledge is dangerous.'

'I know nothing. I swear it. I swear it by the Nine Gods of the Ennead, by the Goddess Maat, by Rē himself.'

Henet was trembling. Her voice had none of its usual whining affected quality. It sounded awed and sincere.

Esa gave a deep sigh. Her figure bent forward. She murmured:

'Help me back to my room.'

Hori and Renisenb came quickly to her.

Esa said: 'Not you, Renisenb. I will have Hori.'

She leaned on him as he helped her from the room towards her own quarters. Glancing up at him she saw his face was stern and unhappy.

She murmured: 'Well, Hori?'

'You have been unwise, Esa, very unwise.'

'I had to know.'

'Yes—but you have taken a terrible risk.'

'I see. So you too think the same?'

'I have thought so for some time, but there is no proof—no shadow of proof. And even now, Esa, *you* have no *proof*. It is all in your mind.'

'It is enough that I *know*.'

'It may be too much.'

'What do you mean? Oh yes, of course.'

'Guard yourself, Esa. From now on you are in danger.'

'We must try and act quickly.'

'That, yes, but what can we do? There must be proof.'

'I know.'

They could say no more. Esa's little maid came running to her mistress. Hori relinquished her to the girl's care and turned away. His face was grave and perplexed.

The little maid chattered and fussed round Esa, but Esa hardly noticed her. She felt old and ill and cold . . . Once again she saw the intent circle of faces watching her as she spoke.

Only a look—a momentary flash of fear and under-standing—could she have been wrong? Was she so sure of what she had seen? After all, her eyes were dim . . .

Yes, she was sure. It was less an expression than the sudden tension of a whole body—a hardening—a rigidity. To one person, and one person only, her rambling words had made sense. That deadly, unerring sense which is truth . . .

CHAPTER 19

Second Month of Summer 15th Day

'Now that the matter is laid before you, Renisenb, what have you to say?'

Renisenb looked doubtfully from her father to Yahmose. Her head felt dull and bemused.

'I do not know.' The words fell from her lips tonelessly.

'Under ordinary conditions,' went on Imhotep, 'there would be plenty of time for discussion. I have other kinsmen, and we could select and reject until we settled upon the most suitable as a husband for you. But as it is uncertain—yes, life is uncertain.'

His voice faltered. He went on:

'That is how the matter stands, Renisenb. Death is facing all three of us today. Yahmose, yourself, myself. At which of us will the peril strike next? Therefore it behoves me to put my affairs in order. If anything should happen to Yahmose you, my only daughter, will need a man to stand by your side and share your inheritance and perform such duties of my estate as cannot be administered by a woman. For who knows at what moment I may be taken from you? The trusteeship and guardianship of Sobek's children I have arranged in my will shall be administered by Hori if Yahmose is no longer alive—also the guardianship of Yahmose's children—since that is his wish—eh, Yahmose?'

Yahmose nodded.

'Hori has always been very close to me. He is as one of my own family.'

'Quite, quite,' said Imhotep. 'But the fact remains he is *not* of the family. Now Kameni is. Therefore, all things considered, he is the best husband available at the moment for Renisenb. So what do you say, Renisenb?'

'I do not know,' Renisenb repeated again.

She felt a terrible lassitude.

'He is handsome and pleasing, you will agree?'

'Oh yes.'

'But you do not want to marry him?' Yahmose asked gently.

Renisenb threw her brother a grateful glance. He was so resolved that she should not be hurried or badgered into doing what she did not want to do.

'I really do not know what I want to do.' She hurried on: 'It is stupid, I know, but I am stupid today. It is—it is the strain under which we are living.'

'With Kameni at your side you will feel protected,' said Imhotep.

Yahmose asked his father: 'Have you considered Hori as a possible husband for Renisenb?'

'Well, yes, it is a possibility . . .'

'His wife died when he was still a young man. Renisenb knows him well and likes him.'

Renisenb sat in a dream while the two men talked. This was her marriage they were discussing, and Yahmose was trying to help her to choose what she herself wanted, but she felt as lifeless as Teti's wooden doll.

Presently she said abruptly, interrupting their speech without even hearing what they were saying:

'I will marry Kameni since you think it is a good thing.'

Imhotep gave an exclamation of satisfaction and hurried out of the hall. Yahmose came over to his sister. He laid a hand on her shoulder.

'Do you want this marriage, Renisenb? Will you be happy?'

'Why should I not be happy? Kameni is handsome and gay and kind.'

'I know.' Yahmose still looked dissatisfied and doubtful. 'But your happiness is important, Renisenb. You must not let my father rush you into something you do not want. You know how he is.'

'Oh yes, yes, when he gets an idea into his head we all have to give way to it.'

'Not necessarily.' Yahmose spoke with firmness. 'I will not give way here unless you wish it.'

'Oh, Yahmose, you never stand out against our father.'

'But I will in this case. He cannot force me to agree with him and I shall not do so.'

Renisenb looked up at him. How resolute and determined his usually undecided face was looking!

'You are good to me, Yahmose,' she said gratefully. 'But indeed I am not yielding to compulsion. The old life here, the life I was so pleased to come back to, has passed away.

Kameni and I will make a new life together and live as a good brother and sister should.'

'If you are sure—'

'I am sure,' said Renisenb, and smiling at him affectionately she went out of the hall on to the porch.

From there she crossed the courtyard. By the edge of the lake Kameni was playing with Teti. Renisenb drew near very quietly and watched them whilst they were still unaware of her approach. Kameni, merry as ever, seemed to be enjoying the game as much as the child did. Renisenb's heart warmed to him. She thought: 'He will make a good father to Teti.'

Then Kameni turned his head and saw her and stood upright with a laugh.

'We have made Teti's doll a ka-priest,' he said. 'And he is making the offerings and attending to the ceremonies at the Tomb.'

'His name is Meriptah,' said Teti. She was very serious.

'He has two children and a scribe like Hori.'

Kameni laughed. 'Teti is very intelligent,' he said. 'And she is strong and beautiful too.'

His eyes went from the child to Renisenb and in their caressing glance Renisenb read the thought of his mind— of the children that she would one day bear him.

It sent a slight thrill through her—yet at the same time a sudden piercing regret. She would have liked in that moment to have seen in his eyes only her own image. She thought: 'Why cannot it be only Renisenb he sees?'

Then the feeling passed and she smiled at him gently.

'My father has spoken to me,' she said.

'And you consent?'

She hesitated a moment before she answered:

'I consent.'

The final word was spoken, that was the end. It was all settled. She wished she did not feel so tired and numb.

'Renisenb?'

'Yes, Kameni.'

'Will you sail with me on the river in a pleasure boat? That is a thing I have always wanted to do with you.'

Odd that he should say that. The very first moment she had seen him she had thought of a square sail and the river and Khay's laughing face. And now she had forgotten Khay's face and in the place of it, against the sail and the river, it would be Kameni who sat and laughed into her eyes.

That was death. That was what death did to you. 'I felt this,' you said, 'I felt that'—but you only said it, you did not now feel anything. The dead were dead. There was no such thing as remembrance . . .

Yes, but there was Teti. There was life and renewing of life, as the waters of the yearly inundation swept away the old and prepared the soil for the new crops.

What had Kait said: 'The women of the household must stand together.' What was she, after all, but a woman of a household—whether Renisenb or another, what matter . . .

Then she heard Kameni's voice—urgent, a little troubled.

'What are you thinking, Renisenb? You go so far away sometimes . . . Will you come with me on the river?'

'Yes, Kameni, I will come with you.'

'We will take Teti too.'

*

It was like a dream, Renisenb thought—the boat and the sail and Kameni and herself and Teti. They had escaped from death and the fear of death. This was the beginning of new life.

Kameni spoke and she answered as though in a trance . . .

'This is my life,' she thought, 'there is no escape . . .'

Then perplexed: 'But why do I say to myself "escape"? What place is there to which I could fly?'

And again there rose before her eyes the little rock chamber beside the Tomb and herself sitting there with one knee drawn up and her chin resting on her hand . . .

She thought: 'But that was something outside life—*this* is life—and there is no escape now until death . . .'

Kameni moored the boat and she stepped ashore. He lifted Teti out. The child clung to him and her hand at his neck broke the string of an amulet he wore. It fell at Renisenb's feet. She picked it up. It was an Ankh sign of electrum and gold.

She gave a little regretful cry. 'It is bent. I am sorry. Be careful—' as Kameni took it from her. 'It may break.'

But his strong fingers, bending it still further, snapped it deliberately in two.

'Oh, what have you done?'

'Take half, Renisenb, and I will take the other. It shall be a sign between us—that we are halves of the same whole.'

He held it out to her, and just as she stretched out her hand to take it, something clicked in her brain and she drew in her breath sharply.

'What is it, Renisenb?'

'Nofret.'

'What do you mean—*Nofret*?'

Renisenb spoke with swift certainty.

'The broken amulet in Nofret's jewel box. It was *you* who gave it to her . . . *You and Nofret* . . . I see everything now. Why she was so unhappy. And I know who put the jewel box in my room. I know everything . . . Do not lie to me, Kameni. I tell you I *know*.'

Kameni made no protest. He stood looking at her steadily and his gaze did not falter. When he spoke, his voice was grave and for once there was no smile on his face.

'I shall not lie to you, Renisenb.'

He waited for a moment, frowning a little as though trying to arrange his thoughts.

'In a way, Renisenb, I am glad that you do know. Though it is not quite as you think.'

'You gave the broken amulet to her—as you would have given it to me—as a sign that you were halves of the same whole. Those were your words.'

'You are angry, Renisenb. I am glad because that shows that you love me. But all the same I must make you understand. I did not give the amulet to Nofret. *She* gave it to *me* . . .'

He paused. 'Perhaps you do not believe me, but it is true. I swear that it is true.'

Renisenb said slowly: 'I will not say that I do not believe you . . . That may very well be true.'

Nofret's dark, unhappy face rose up before her eyes.

Kameni was going on, eagerly, boyishly . . .

'Try and understand, Renisenb. Nofret was very beautiful.

215

I was flattered and pleased—who would not be? But I never really loved her—'

Renisenb felt an odd pang of pity. No, Kameni had not loved Nofret—but Nofret had loved Kameni—had loved him despairingly and bitterly. It was at just this spot on the Nile bank that she had spoken to Nofret that morning, offering her friendship and affection. She remembered only too well the dark tide of hate and misery that had emanated from the girl then. The cause of it was clear enough now. Poor Nofret—the concubine of a fussy, elderly man, eating her heart out for love of a gay, careless, handsome young man who had cared little or nothing for her.

Kameni was going on eagerly.

'Do you not understand, Renisenb, that as soon as I came here, I saw you and loved you? That from that moment I thought of no one else? Nofret saw it plainly enough.'

Yes, Renisenb thought, Nofret had seen it. Nofret had hated her from that moment—and Renisenb did not feel inclined to blame her.

'I did not even want to write the letter to your father. I did not want to have anything to do with Nofret's schemes any more. But it was difficult—you must try and realize that it was difficult.'

'Yes, yes,' Renisenb spoke impatiently. 'All that does not matter. It is only Nofret that matters. She was very unhappy. She loved you, I think, very much.'

'Well, I did not love her.' Kameni spoke impatiently.

'You are cruel,' said Renisenb.

'No, I am a man, that is all. If a woman chooses to

make herself miserable about me, it annoys me, that is the simple truth. I did not want Nofret. I wanted you. Oh, Renisenb, you cannot be angry with me for *that*?'

In spite of herself she smiled.

'Do not let Nofret who is dead make trouble between us who are living. I love you, Renisenb, and you love me and that is all that matters.'

Yes, Renisenb thought, that is all that matters . . .

She looked at Kameni who stood with his head a little on one side, a pleading expression on his gay, confident face. He looked very young.

Renisenb thought: 'He is right. Nofret is dead and we are alive. I understand her hatred of me now—and I am sorry that she suffered—but it was not my fault. And it was not Kameni's fault that he loved me and not her. These things happen.'

Teti, who had been playing on the river bank, came up and pulled her mother's hand.

'Shall we go home now? Mother—shall we go home?'

Renisenb gave a deep sigh.

'Yes,' she said, 'we will go home.'

They walked towards the house, Teti running a little way in front of them. Kameni gave a sigh of satisfaction.

'You are generous, Renisenb, as well as lovely. All is the same as it was between us?'

'Yes, Kameni. All the same.'

He lowered his voice. 'Out there on the river—I was very happy. Were you happy too, Renisenb?'

'Yes, I was happy.'

'You looked happy. But you looked as though you were

217

thinking of something very far away. I want you to think of *me*.'

'I was thinking of you.'

He took her hand and she did not draw it away. He sang very softly under his breath:

'*My sister is like the persea tree . . .*'

He felt her hand tremble in his and heard the quickened pace of her breathing and was satisfied at last . . .

Renisenb called Henet to her room.

Henet, hurrying in, came to an abrupt stop as she saw Renisenb standing by the open jewel box with the broken amulet in her hand. Renisenb's face was stern and angry.

'You put this jewel box in my room, didn't you, Henet? You wanted me to find that amulet. You wanted me one day—'

'To find out who had the other half? I see you have found out. Well, it's always as well to know, isn't it, Renisenb?'

Henet laughed spitefully.

'You wanted the knowledge to hurt me,' said Renisenb, her anger still at white heat. 'You like hurting people, don't you, Henet? You never say anything straight out. You wait and wait—until the best moment comes. You hate us all, don't you? You always have.'

'The things you're saying, Renisenb! I'm sure you don't mean them!'

But there was no whine in Henet's voice now, only a sly triumph.

'You wanted to make trouble between me and Kameni. Well, there is no trouble.'

'That's very nice and forgiving of you, I'm sure, Renisenb. You're quite different from Nofret, aren't you?'

'Do not let us talk of Nofret.'

'No, better not perhaps. Kameni's lucky as well as being good-looking, isn't he? It was lucky for him, I mean, that Nofret died when she did. She could have made a lot of trouble for him. With your father. She wouldn't have liked his marrying you—no, she wouldn't have liked it at all. In fact, I think she would have found some way of stopping it. I'm quite sure she would.'

Renisenb looked at her with cold dislike.

'There is always poison in your tongue, Henet. It stings like a scorpion. But you cannot make me unhappy.'

'Well, that's splendid, isn't it? You must be very much in love. Oh, he's a handsome young man is Kameni—and he knows how to sing a very pretty love song. He'll always get what he wants, never fear. I admire him, I really do. He always seems so simple and straightforward.'

'What are you trying to say, Henet?'

'I'm just telling you that I admire Kameni. And I'm quite sure that he *is* simple and straightforward. It's not put on. The whole thing is quite like one of those tales the storytellers in the Bazaars recite. The poor young scribe marrying the master's daughter and sharing the inheritance with her and living happily ever afterwards. Wonderful what good luck a handsome young man always has.'

'I am right,' said Renisenb. 'You do hate us.'

'Now how can you say that, Renisenb, when you know how I've slaved for you all ever since your mother died?'

But there was still the evil triumph in Henet's voice rather than the customary whine.

Renisenb looked down again at the jewel box and suddenly another certainty came into her mind.

'It was *you* who put the gold lion necklace in this box. Don't deny it, Henet. I know, I tell you.'

Henet's sly triumph died. She looked suddenly frightened.

'I couldn't help it, Renisenb. I was afraid . . .'

'What do you mean—afraid?'

Henet came a step nearer and lowered her voice.

'*She* gave it to me—Nofret, I mean. Oh, some time before she died. She gave me one or two—presents. Nofret was generous, you know. Oh yes, she was always generous.'

'I daresay she paid you well.'

'That's not a nice way of putting it, Renisenb. But I'm telling you all about it. She gave me the gold lion necklace and an amethyst clasp and one or two other things. And then, when that boy came out with his story of having seen a woman with that necklace on—well, I was afraid. I thought maybe they'd think that it was *I* who poisoned Yahmose's wine. So I put the necklace in the box.'

'Is that the truth, Henet? Do you ever speak the truth?'

'I swear it's the truth, Renisenb. I was afraid . . .'

Renisenb looked at her curiously. 'You're shaking, Henet. You look as though you were afraid now.'

'Yes, I am afraid . . . I've reason to be.'

'Why? Tell me.'

Henet licked her thin lips. She glanced sideways, behind her. Her eyes came back like a hunted animal's.

'Tell me,' said Renisenb.

Henet shook her head. She said in an uncertain voice: 'There's nothing to tell.'

'You know too much, Henet. You've always known too much. You've enjoyed it, but now it's dangerous. That's it, isn't it?'

Henet shook her head again. Then she laughed maliciously.

'You wait, Renisenb. One day I shall hold the whip in this house—and crack it. Wait and see.'

Renisenb drew herself up. 'You will not harm *me*, Henet. My mother will not let you harm me.'

Henet's face changed—the eyes burned.

'I hated your mother,' she said. 'I always hated her . . . And you who have her eyes—and her voice—her beauty and her arrogance—I hate *you*, Renisenb.'

Renisenb laughed. 'And at last—I've made you say it!'

CHAPTER 20

Second Month of Summer 15th Day

Old Esa limped wearily into her room.

She was perplexed and very weary. Age, she realized, was at last taking toll of her. So far she had acknowledged her weariness of body, but had been conscious of no weariness of mind. But now she had to admit that the strain of remaining mentally alert was taxing her bodily resources.

If she knew now, as she believed she did, from what quarter danger impended—yet that knowledge permitted of no mental relaxation. Instead she had to be more than ever on her guard since she had deliberately drawn attention to herself. Proof—proof—she must get proof . . . But how?

It was there, she realized, that her age told against her. She was too tired to improvise—to make the mental creative effort. All she was capable of was defence—to remain alert, watchful, guarding herself.

For the killer—she had no illusions about that—would be quite ready to kill again.

Well, she had no intention of being the next victim.

Poison, she felt sure, was the vehicle that would be employed. Violence was not conceivable since she was never alone, but was always surrounded by servants. So it would be poison. Well, she could counter that. Renisenb should cook her food and bring it to her. She had a wine stand and jar brought to her room and after a slave had tasted it, she waited twenty-four hours to make sure that no evil results followed. She made Renisenb share her food and her wine—although she had no fear for Renisenb—yet. It might be that there was no fear for Renisenb—ever. But of that one could not be sure.

Between whiles she sat motionless, driving her weary brain to devise means of proving the truth or watching her little maid starching and pleating her linen dresses, or re-stringing necklaces and bracelets. This evening she was very weary. She had joined Imhotep at his request to discuss the question of Renisenb's marriage before he himself spoke to his daughter.

Imhotep, shrunken and fretful, was a shadow of his former self. His manner had lost its pomposity and assurance. He leaned now on his mother's indomitable will and determination.

As for Esa, she had been fearful—very fearful—of saying the wrong thing. Lives might hang on an injudicious word.

Yes, she said at last, the idea of marriage was wise. And there was no time to go far afield for a husband amongst more important members of the family clan. After all, the female line was the important one—her husband would be only the administrator of the inheritance that came to Renisenb and Renisenb's children.

Agatha Christie

So it came to a question of Hori—a man of integrity, of old and long-approved friendship, the son of a small land-owner whose estate had adjoined their own, or young Kameni with his claims of cousinship.

Esa had weighed the matter carefully before speaking. A false word now—and disaster might result.

Then she had made her answer, stressing it with the force of her indomitable personality. Kameni, she said, was undoubtedly the husband for Renisenb. Their declarations and the necessary attendant festivities—much curtailed owing to the recent bereavements—might take place in a week's time. That is, if Renisenb was willing. Kameni was a fine young man—together they would raise strong children. Moreover the two of them loved one another.

Well, Esa thought, she had cast her die. The thing would be pegged out now on the gaming board. It was out of her hands. She had done what she thought expedient. If it was hazardous—well, Esa liked a match at the gaming board quite as well as Ipy had done. Life was not a matter of safety—it must be hazarded to win the game.

She looked suspiciously round her room when she returned to it. Particularly she examined the big wine jar. It was covered over and sealed as she had left it. She always sealed it when she left the room and the seal hung safely round her neck.

Yes—she was taking no risks of that kind. Esa chuckled with malicious satisfaction. Not so easy to kill an old woman. Old women knew the value of life—and knew most of the tricks too. Tomorrow—She called her little maid.

'Where is Hori? Do you know?'

The girl replied that she thought Hori was up at the Tomb in the rock chamber.

Esa nodded satisfaction.

'Go up to him there. Tell him that tomorrow morning, when Imhotep and Yahmose are out on the cultivation, taking Kameni with them for the counting, and when Kait is at the lake with the children, he is to come to me here. Have you understood that? Repeat it.'

The little maid did so, and Esa sent her off.

Yes, her plan was satisfactory. The consultation with Hori would be quite private since she would send Henet on an errand to the weaving sheds. She would warn Hori of what was to come and they could speak freely together.

When the black girl returned with the message that Hori would do as she said, Esa gave a sigh of relief.

Now, these things settled, her weariness spread over her like a flood. She told the girl to bring the pot of sweet smelling ointment and massage her limbs.

The rhythm soothed her, and the unguent eased the aching of her bones.

She stretched herself out at last, her head on the wooden pillow, and slept—her fears for the moment allayed.

She woke much later with a strange sensation of cold-ness. Her feet, her hands, were numbed and dead . . . It was like a constriction stealing all over the body. She could feel it numbing her brain, paralysing her will, slowing down the beat of her heart.

She thought: 'This is Death . . .'

A strange death—death unheralded, with no warning signs.

This, she thought, is how the old die . . .

And then a surer conviction came to her. This was *not* natural death! This was the Enemy striking out of the darkness.

Poison . . .

But how? When? All she had eaten, all she had drunk—tested, secured—there had been no loophole of error.

Then how? When?

With her last feeble flickers of intelligence, Esa sought to penetrate the mystery. She must know—she *must*—before she died.

She felt the pressure increasing on her heart—the deadly coldness—the slow painful indrawing of her breath.

How had the enemy done this thing?

And suddenly, from the past, a fleeting memory came to aid her understanding. The shaven skin of a lamb—a lump of smelling grease—an experiment of her father's—to show that some poisons could be absorbed by the skin. Wool fat—unguents made of wool fat. That was how the enemy had reached her. Her pot of sweet smelling unguent, so necessary to an Egyptian woman. The poison had been in that . . .

And tomorrow—Hori—he would not know—she could not tell him . . . It was too late.

In the morning a frightened little slave girl went running through the house crying out that her lady had died in her sleep.

Imhotep stood looking down on Esa's body. His face was sorrowful, but not suspicious.

His mother, he said, had died naturally enough of old age.

'She was old,' he said. 'Yes, she was old. It was doubtless time for her to go to Osiris, and all her troubles and sorrows have hastened the end. But it seems to have come peacefully enough. Thank Rē in his mercy that here is a death unaided by man or by evil spirit. There is no violence here. See how peaceful she looks.'

Renisenb wept and Yahmose comforted her. Henet went about sighing and shaking her head, and saying what a loss Esa would be and how devoted she, Henet, had always been to her. Kameni checked his singing and showed a proper mourning face.

Hori came and stood looking down at the dead woman. It was the hour of her summons to him. He wondered what, exactly, she had meant to say.

She had had something definite to tell him.

Now he would never know.

But he thought, perhaps, that he could guess . . .

CHAPTER 21

Second Month of Summer 16th Day

'Hori—was she killed?'

'I think so, Renisenb.'

'How?'

'I do not know.'

'But she was so careful.' The girl's voice was distressed and bewildered. 'She was always on the watch. She took every precaution. Everything she ate and drank was proved and tested.'

'I know, Renisenb. But all the same I think she was killed.'

'And she was the wisest of us all—the cleverest! She was sure that no harm could befall her. Hori, it *must* be magic! Evil magic, the spell of an evil spirit.'

'You believe that because it is the easiest thing to believe. People are like that. But Esa herself would not have believed it. If she knew—before she died, and did not die in her sleep—she knew it was living person's work.'

'And she knew whose?'

'Yes. She had shown her suspicion too openly. She became

a danger to the enemy. The fact that she died proves that her suspicion was correct.'

'And she told you—who it was?'

'No,' said Hori. 'She did not tell me. She never mentioned a name. Nevertheless, her thought and my thought were, I am convinced, the same.'

'Then you must tell *me*, Hori, so that I may be on my guard.'

'No, Renisenb, I care too much for your safety to do that.'

'Am I so safe?'

Hori's face darkened. He said: 'No, Renisenb, you are not safe. No one is safe. But you are much safer than if you were assured of the truth—for then you would become a definite menace to be removed at once whatever the risk.'

'What about you, Hori? *You* know.'

He corrected her. 'I *think* I know. But I have said nothing and shown nothing. Esa was unwise. She spoke out. She showed the direction in which her thoughts were tending. She should not have done that—I told her so afterwards.'

'But you—Hori . . . If anything happens to you . . .'

She stopped. She was aware of Hori's eyes looking into hers.

Grave, intent, seeing straight into her mind and heart . . . He took her hands in his and held them lightly.

'Do not fear for me, little Renisenb . . . All will be well.'

Yes, she thought, all will indeed be well if Hori says so. Strange, that feeling of content, of peace, of clear singing happiness . . . As lovely and as remote as the far distance seen from the Tomb—a distance in which there was no clamour of human demands and restrictions.

Suddenly, almost harshly, she heard herself saying:

'I am to marry Kameni.'

Hori let her hands go—quietly and quite naturally.

'I know, Renisenb.'

'They—my father—they think it is the best thing.'

'I know.'

He moved away.

The courtyard walls seemed to come nearer, the voices within the house and from the cornbins outside sounded louder and noisier.

Renisenb had only one thought in her mind: 'Hori is going . . .'

She called to him timidly:

'Hori, where are you going?'

'Out to the fields with Yahmose. There is much work there to be done and recorded. The reaping is nearly finished.'

'And Kameni?'

'Kameni comes with us.'

Renisenb cried out: 'I am afraid here. Yes, even in daylight with all the servants all round and Rē sailing across the Heavens, I am afraid.'

He came quickly back.

'Do not be afraid, Renisenb. I swear to you that you need not be afraid. Not today.'

'But after today?'

'Today is enough to live through—and I swear to you you are not in danger today.'

Renisenb looked at him and frowned.

'But we *are* in danger? Yahmose, my father, myself? It is not *I* who am threatened first . . . is that what you think?'

'Try not to think about it, Renisenb. I am doing all I can, though it may appear to you that I am doing nothing.'

'I see—' Renisenb looked at him thoughtfully. 'Yes, I see. It is to be Yahmose first. The enemy has tried twice with poison and failed. There is to be a third attempt. That is why you will be close beside him—to protect him. And after that it will be the turn of my father and myself. Who is there who hates our family so much that—'

'Hush. You would do well not to talk of these things. Trust me, Renisenb. Try and banish fear from your mind.'

Renisenb threw her head back. She faced him proudly.

'I do trust you, Hori. You will not let me die . . . I love life very much and I do not want to leave it.'

'You shall not leave it, Renisenb.'

'Nor you either, Hori.'

'Nor I either.'

They smiled at each other and then Hori went away to find Yahmose.

Renisenb sat back on her haunches watching Kait.

Kait was helping the children to model toys out of clay, using the water of the lake. Her fingers were busy kneading and shaping and her voice encouraged the two small serious boys at their task. Kait's face was the same as usual, affectionate, plain, expressionless. The surrounding atmosphere

of violent death and constant fear seemed to affect her not
at all . . .

Hori had bidden Renisenb not to think, but with the
best will in the world Renisenb could not obey. If Hori
knew the enemy, if Esa had known the enemy, then there
was no reason why she should not know the enemy too.
She might be safer unknowing, but no human creature
could be content to have it that way. She wanted to know.

And it must be very easy—very easy indeed. Her father,
clearly, could not desire to kill his own children. So that
left—who did it leave? It left, starkly and uncompromisingly,
two people, Kait and Henet.

Women, both of them . . .

And surely with no reason for killing . . .

Yet Henet hated them all . . . Yes, undoubtedly Henet
hated them. She had admitted hating Renisenb. So why
should she not hate the others equally?

Renisenb tried to project herself into the dim, tortured
recesses of Henet's brain. Living here, all these years,
working, protesting her devotion, lying, spying, making
mischief . . . Coming here, long ago, as the poor relative
of a great and beautiful lady. Seeing that lovely lady happy
with husband and children. Repudiated by her own
husband, her only child dead . . . Yes, that might be the
way of it. Like a wound from a spear thrust that Renisenb
had once seen. It had healed quickly over the surface, but
beneath evil matters had festered and raged and the arm
had swollen and had gone hard to the touch. And then
the physician had come and, with a suitable incantation,
had plunged a small knife into the hard, swollen, distorted

limb. It had been like the breaking down of an irrigation dyke. A great stream of evil smelling stuff had come welling out . . .

That, perhaps, was like Henet's mind. Sorrow and injury smoothed over too quickly—and festering poison beneath, ever swelling in a great tide of hate and venom.

But did Henet hate Imhotep too? Surely not. For years she had fluttered round him, fawning on him, flattering him . . . He believed in her implicitly. Surely that devotion could not be wholly feigned?

And if she were devoted to him, could she deliberately inflict all this sorrow and loss upon him?

Ah, but suppose she hated him too—had always hated him. Had flattered him deliberately with a view to bringing out his weakness? Supposing Imhotep was the one she hated *most*? Then to a distorted, evil-ridden mind, what better pleasure could there be than this? To let him see his children die off one by one . . .

'What is the matter, Renisenb?' Kait was staring at her. 'You look so strange.'

Renisenb stood up.

'I feel as though I were going to vomit,' she said.

In a sense it was true enough. The picture she had been conjuring up induced in her a strong feeling of nausea. Kait accepted the words at their face value.

'You have eaten too many green dates—or perhaps the fish had turned.'

'No, no, it is nothing I have eaten. It is the terrible thing we are living through.'

'Oh, that.'

Kait's disclaimer was so nonchalant that Renisenb stared at her.

'But, Kait, are you not afraid?'

'No, I do not think so.' Kait considered. 'If anything happens to Imhotep, the children will be protected by Hori. Hori is honest. He will guard their inheritance for them.'

'Yahmose will do that.'

'Yahmose will die, too.'

'Kait, you say that so calmly. Do you not mind at all? I mean, that my father and Yahmose should die?'

Kait considered for a moment or two. Then she shrugged her shoulders.

'We are two women together—let us be honest. Imhotep I have always considered tyrannical and unfair. He behaved outrageously in the matter of his concubine—letting himself be persuaded by her to disinherit his own flesh and blood. I have never liked Imhotep. As to Yahmose, he is nothing. Satipy ruled him in every way. Lately, since she is gone, he takes authority on himself, gives orders. He would always prefer his children before mine—that is natural. So, if he is to die, it is as well for my children that it should be so—that is how I see it. Hori has no children and he is just. All these happenings have been upsetting—but I have been thinking lately that very likely they are all for the best.'

'You can talk like that, Kait—so calmly, so coldly? When your own husband, whom you loved, was the first to be killed?'

A faint expression of some indefinable nature passed over Kait's face. She gave Renisenb a glance which seemed to contain a certain scornful irony.

'You are very like Teti sometimes, Renisenb. Really, one would swear, no older!'

'You do not mourn for Sobek.' Renisenb spoke the words slowly. 'No, I have noticed that.'

'Come, Renisenb, I fulfilled all the conventions. I know how a newly made widow should behave.'

'Yes—that was all there was to it . . . So—it means—that you did not love Sobek?'

Kait shrugged her shoulders.

'Why should I?'

'Kait! He was your husband—he gave you children.'

Kait's expression softened. She looked down at the two small boys engrossed with the clay and then to where Ankh was rolling about chanting to herself and waving her little legs.

'Yes, he gave me my children. For that I thank him. But what was he, after all? A handsome braggart—a man who was always going to other women. He did not take a sister, decently, into the household, some modest person who would have been useful to us all. No, he went to ill-famed houses, spending much copper and gold there, drinking too and asking for all the most expensive dancing girls. It was fortunate that Imhotep kept him as short as he did and that he had to account so closely for the sales he made on the estate. What love and respect should I have for a man like that? And what are men anyway? They are necessary to breed children, that is all. But the strength of the race is in the women. It is *we*, Renisenb, who hand down to our children all that is ours. As for men, let them breed and die early . . .'

Agatha Christie

The scorn and contempt in Kait's voice rose in a note like some musical instrument. Her strong, ugly face was transfigured.

Renisenb thought with dismay:

'Kait is strong. If she is stupid, it is with a stupidity that is satisfied with itself. She hates and despises men. I should have known. Once before I caught a glimpse of this—this *menacing* quality. Yes, Kait is strong—'

Unthinkingly, Renisenb's gaze fell to Kait's hands. They were squeezing and kneading clay—strong, muscular hands, and as Renisenb watched them pushing down the clay, she thought of Ipy and of strong hands pushing his head down into the water and holding it there inexorably. Yes, Kait's hands could have done that . . .

The little girl, Ankh, rolled over on to a thorny spine and set up a wail. Kait rushed to her. She picked her up, holding her to her breast, crooning over her. Her face now was all love and tenderness. Henet came running out from the porch.

'Is anything wrong? The child yelled so loud. I thought perhaps—'

She paused, disappointed. Her eager, mean, spiteful face, hoping for some catastrophe, fell.

Renisenb looked from one woman to the other.

Hate in one face. Love in the other. Which, she wondered, was the more terrible?

'Yahmose, be careful, be careful of Kait.'

'Of Kait?' Yahmose showed his astonishment. 'My dear Renisenb—'

'I tell you, she is dangerous.'

'Our quiet Kait? She has always been a meek, submissive woman, not very clever—'

Renisenb interrupted him.

'She is neither meek nor submissive. I am afraid of her, Yahmose. I want you to be on your guard.'

'Against Kait?' He was still incredulous. 'I can hardly see Kait dealing out death all round. She would not have the brains.'

'I do not think that it is brains that are concerned. A knowledge of poisons, that is all that has been needed. And you know that such knowledge is often found amongst certain families. They hand it down from mother to daughter. They brew these concoctions themselves from potent herbs. It is the kind of lore that Kait might easily have. She brews medicines for the children when they are ill, you know.'

'Yes, that is true.' Yahmose spoke thoughtfully.

'Henet too is an evil woman,' went on Renisenb.

'Henet—yes. We have never liked her. In fact, but for my father's protection—'

'Our father is deceived in her,' said Renisenb.

'That may well be.' Yahmose added in a matter-of-fact tone, 'She flatters him.'

Renisenb looked at him for a moment in surprise. It was the first time she had ever heard Yahmose utter a sentence containing criticism of Imhotep. He had always seemed overawed by his father.

But now, she realized, Yahmose was gradually taking the lead. Imhotep had aged by years in the last few weeks.

He was incapable now of giving orders, of taking decisions. Even his physical activity seemed impaired. He spent long hours staring in front of him, his eyes filmed and abstracted. Sometimes he seemed not to understand what was said to him.

'Do you think that she—' Renisenb stopped. She looked round and began, 'Is it she, do you think, who has—who is—?'

Yahmose caught her by the arm.

'Be quiet, Renisenb, these things are better not said—not even whispered.'

'Then you too think—'

Yahmose said softly and urgently:

'Say nothing now. We have plans.'

CHAPTER 22

Second Month of Summer 17th Day

The following day was the festival of the new moon. Imhotep was forced to go up to the Tomb, to make the offerings. Yahmose begged his father to leave it to him on this occasion, but Imhotep was obdurate. With what seemed now a feeble parody of his old manner, he murmured, 'Unless I see to things myself, how can I be sure they are properly done? Have I ever shirked my duties? Have I not provided for all of you, supported you all—'

His voice stopped. 'All? *All*—? Ah, I forget—my two brave sons—my handsome Sobek—my clever and beloved Ipy. Gone from me. Yahmose and Renisenb—my dear son and daughter—you are still with me—but for how long—how long . . .'

'Many long years, we hope,' said Yahmose.

He spoke rather loudly as to a deaf man.

'Eh? What?' Imhotep seemed to have fallen into a coma. He said suddenly and surprisingly:

'It depends on Henet, does it not? Yes, it depends on Henet.'

Yahmose and Renisenb exchanged glances.

Renisenb said gently and clearly:

'I do not understand you, father?'

Imhotep muttered something they did not catch. Then, raising his voice, a little, but with dull and vacant eyes, he said:

'Henet understands me. She always has. She knows how great my responsibilities are—how great . . . Yes, how great . . . And always ingratitude . . . Therefore there must be retribution. That, I think, is a practice well established. Presumption must be punished. Henet has always been modest, humble and devoted. She shall be rewarded . . .'

He drew himself up and said pompously:

'You understand, Yahmose. Henet is to have all she wants. Her commands are to be obeyed!'

'But why is this, father?'

'Because I say so. Because, if what Henet wants is done, there will be no more deaths . . .'

He nodded his head sagely and went away—leaving Yahmose and Renisenb staring at each other in wonder and alarm.

'What does this mean, Yahmose?'

'I do not know, Renisenb. Sometimes I think my father no longer knows what he does or says . . .'

'No—perhaps not. But I think, Yahmose, that *Henet* knows very well what she is saying and doing. She said to me, only the other day, that it would soon be *she* who would crack the whip in this house.'

They looked at each other. Then Yahmose put his hand on Renisenb's arm.

'Do not anger her. You show your feelings too plainly, Renisenb. You heard what my father said? If what Henet wants is done—*there will be no more deaths . . .*'

Henet was crouching down on her haunches in one of the store rooms counting out piles of sheets. They were old sheets and she held the mark on the corner of one close up to her eyes.

'Ashayet,' she murmured. 'Ashayet's sheets. Marked with the year she came here—she and I together . . . That's a long time ago. Do you know, I wonder, what your sheets are being used for now, Ashayet?'

She broke off in the midst of a chuckle, and gave a start as a sound made her glance over her shoulder.

It was Yahmose.

'What are you doing, Henet?'

'The embalmers need more sheets. Piles and piles of sheets they've used. Four hundred cubits they used yesterday alone. It's terrible the way these funerals use up the sheeting! We'll have to use these old ones. They're good quality and not much worn. Your mother's sheets, Yahmose—yes, your mother's sheets . . .'

'Who said you might take those?'

Henet laughed.

'Imhotep's given everything into my charge. I don't have to ask leave. He trusts poor old Henet. He knows she'll see to everything in the right way. I've seen to most things in this house for a long time. I think—now—I'm going to have my reward!'

'It looks like it, Henet.' Yahmose's tone was mild. 'My father said,' he paused, *'everything depends on you.'*

'Did he now? Well that's nice hearing—but perhaps *you* don't think so, Yahmose.'

'Well—I'm not quite sure.' Yahmose's tone was still mild, but he watched her closely.

'I think you'd better agree with your father, Yahmose. We don't want any more—*trouble*, do we?'

'I don't quite understand. You mean—we don't want any more deaths?'

'There are going to be more deaths, Yahmose. Oh yes—'

'Who is going to die next, Henet?'

'Why do you think I should know that?'

'Because I think you know a great deal. You knew the other day, for instance, that Ipy was going to die . . . You are very clever, aren't you, Henet?'

Henet bridled.

'So you're beginning to realize that now! I'm not poor, stupid Henet any longer. I'm the one who *knows*.'

'What do you know, Henet?'

Henet's voice changed. It was low and sharp.

'I know that *at last* I can do as I choose in this house. There will be no one to stop me. Imhotep leans upon me already. And *you* will do the same, eh, Yahmose?'

'And Renisenb?'

Henet laughed, a malicious, happy chuckle.

'Renisenb will not be here.'

'You think it is Renisenb who will die next?'

'What do *you* think, Yahmose?'

'I am waiting to hear what *you* say.'

242

'Perhaps I only meant that Renisenb will marry—and go away.'

'What *do* you mean, Henet?'

Henet chuckled.

'Esa once said my tongue was dangerous. Perhaps it is!'

She laughed shrilly, swaying to and fro on her heels.

'Well, Yahmose, what do you say? Am I at last to do as I choose in this house?'

Yahmose studied her for a moment before saying:

'Yes, Henet. You are so clever. You shall do as you choose.'

He turned to meet Hori who was coming from the main hall and who said: 'There you are, Yahmose. Imhotep is awaiting you. It is time to go up to the Tomb.'

Yahmose nodded.

'I am coming.' He lowered his voice. 'Hori—I think Henet is mad—she is definitely afflicted by the devils. I begin to believe that *she* has been responsible for all these happenings.'

Hori paused a moment before saying in his quiet, detached voice:

'She is a strange woman—and an evil one, I think.'

Yahmose lowered his voice still more:

'Hori, I think Renisenb is in danger.'

'From Henet?'

'Yes. She has just hinted that Renisenb may be the next to—go.'

Imhotep's voice came fretfully:

'Am I to wait all day? What conduct is this? No one considers me any more. No one knows what I suffer. Where is Henet? Henet understands.'

Agatha Christie

From within the storeroom Henet's chuckle of triumph came shrilly.

'Do you hear that, Yahmose? Henet! Henet is the one!'

Yahmose said quietly:

'Yes, Henet—I understand. You are the powerful one. You and my father and I—we three together . . .'

Hori went off to find Imhotep. Yahmose spoke a few more words to Henet who nodded, her face sparkling with malicious triumph.

Then Yahmose joined Hori and Imhotep, apologizing for his delay, and the three men went up to the Tomb together.

The day passed slowly for Renisenb.

She was restless, passing to and fro from the house to the porch, then to the lake and then back again to the house.

At midday Imhotep returned, and after a meal had been served to him, he came out upon the porch and Renisenb joined him.

She sat with her hands clasped round her knees, occasionally looking up at her father's face. It still wore that absent, bewildered expression. Imhotep spoke little. Once or twice he sighed deeply.

Once he roused himself and asked for Henet. But just at that time Henet had gone with linen to the embalmers.

Renisenb asked her father where Hori and Yahmose were.

'Hori has gone out to the flax fields. There is a tally to

be taken there. Yahmose is on the cultivation. It all falls on him now . . . Alas for Sobek and Ipy! My boys—my handsome boys . . .'

Renisenb tried quickly to distract him.

'Cannot Kameni oversee the workers?'

'Kameni? Who is Kameni? I have no son of that name.'

'Kameni the scribe. Kameni who is to be my husband.'

He stared at her.

'You, Renisenb? But you are to marry Khay.'

She sighed, but said no more. It seemed cruel to try and bring him back to the present. After a little while, however, he roused himself and exclaimed suddenly:

'Of course. Kameni! He has gone to give some instructions to the overseer at the brewery. I must go and join him.'

He strode away, muttering to himself, but with resumption of his old manner, so that Renisenb felt a little cheered.

Perhaps this clouding of his brain was only temporary.

She looked round her. There seemed something sinister about the silence of the house and court today. The children were at the far side of the lake. Kait was not with them and Renisenb wondered where she was.

Then Henet came out on to the porch. She looked round her and then came sidling up to Renisenb. She had resumed her old wheedling, humble manner.

'I've been waiting till I could get you alone, Renisenb.'

'Why, Henet?'

Henet lowered her voice.

'I've got a message for you—from Hori.'

Agatha Christie

'What does he say?' Renisenb's voice was eager.

'He asks that you should go up to the Tomb.'

'Now?'

'No. Be there an hour before sunset. That was the message. If he is not there then, he asks that you will wait until he comes. It is important, he says.'

Henet paused—and then added:

'I was to wait until I got you alone to say this—and no one was to overhear.'

Henet glided away.

Renisenb felt her spirits lightened. She felt glad at the prospect of going up to the peace and quietness of the Tomb. Glad that she would see Hori and be able to talk to him freely. The only thing that surprised her a little was that he should have entrusted his message to Henet.

Nevertheless, malicious though Henet was, she had delivered the message faithfully.

'And why should I fear Henet at any time?' thought Renisenb. 'I am stronger than she is.'

She drew herself up proudly. She felt young and confident and very much alive . . .

After giving the message to Renisenb, Henet went once more into the linen storeroom. She was laughing quietly to herself.

She bent over the disordered piles of sheets.

'We'll be needing more of you soon,' she said to them gleefully. 'Do you hear, Ashayet? I'm the mistress here now and I'm telling you that your linen will bandage yet another body. And whose body is that, do you think? Hee hee! You've not been able to do much about things, have you? You and your mother's brother, the Nomarch! Justice? What justice can you do in *this* world? Answer me that!'

There was a movement behind the bales of linen. Henet half-turned her head.

Then a great width of linen was thrown over her, stifling her mouth and nose. An inexorable hand wound the fabric round and round her body, swathing her like a corpse until her struggles ceased . . .

CHAPTER 23

Second Month of Summer 17th Day

Renisenb sat in the entrance of the rock chamber, staring out at the Nile and lost in a queer dream fantasy of her own.

It seemed to her a very long time since the day when she had first sat here, soon after her return to her father's house. That had been the day when she had declared so gaily that everything was unchanged, that all in the home was exactly as it had been when she left it eight years before.

She remembered now how Hori had told her that she herself was not the same Renisenb who had gone away with Khay and how she had answered confidently that she soon would be.

Then Hori had gone on to speak of changes that came from within, of a rottenness that left no outward sign.

She knew now something of what had been in his mind when he said those things. He had been trying to prepare her. She had been so assured, so blind—accepting so easily the outward values of her family.

It had taken Nofret's coming to open her eyes . . .

Yes, Nofret's coming. It had all hinged on that.

With Nofret had come death . . .

Whether Nofret had been evil or not, she had certainly brought evil . . .

And the evil was still in their midst.

For the last time, Renisenb played with the belief that Nofret's spirit was the cause of everything . . .

Nofret, malicious and dead . . .

Or Henet, malicious and living . . . Henet the despised, the sycophantic, fawning Henet . . .

Renisenb shivered, stirred, and then slowly rose to her feet.

She could wait for Hori no longer. The sun was on the point of setting. Why, she wondered, had he not come?

She got up, glanced round her and started to descend the path to the valley below.

It was very quiet at this evening hour. Quiet and beautiful, she thought. What had delayed Hori? If he had come, they would at least have had this hour together . . .

There would not be many such hours. In the near future, when she was Kameni's wife—

Was she really going to marry Kameni? With a kind of shock Renisenb shook herself free from the mood of dull acquiescence that had held her so long. She felt like a sleeper awakening from a feverish dream. Caught in that stupor of fear and uncertainty she had assented to whatever had been proposed to her.

But now she was Renisenb again, and if she married

Kameni it would be because she wanted to marry him, and not because her family arranged it. Kameni with his handsome, laughing face! She loved him, didn't she? That was why she was going to marry him.

In this evening hour up here, there was clarity and truth. No confusion. She was Renisenb, walking here above the world, serene and unafraid, herself at last.

Had she not once said to Hori that she must walk down this path alone at the hour of Nofret's death? That whether fear went with her or not, she must still go alone.

Well, she was doing it now. This was just about the hour when she and Satipy had bent over Nofret's body. And it was about this same hour when Satipy in her turn had walked down the path and had suddenly looked back—to see doom overtaking her.

At just about this same point too. What was it that Satipy had heard, to make her look suddenly behind her?

Footsteps?

Footsteps . . . but Renisenb heard footsteps now *following her down the path*.

Her heart gave a sudden leap of fear. It *was* true, then! Nofret was behind her, following her . . .

Fear coursed through her, but her footsteps did not slacken. Nor did they race ahead. She must overcome fear, since there was, in her mind, no evil deed to regret . . .

She steadied herself, gathered her courage and, still walking, turned her head.

Then she felt a great throb of relief. It was Yahmose following her. No spirit from the dead, but her own brother. He must have been busied in the offering chamber of the Tomb and have come out of it just after she had passed.

She stopped with a happy little cry.

'Oh Yahmose, I'm so glad it's you.'

He was coming up to her rapidly. She was just beginning another sentence—a recital of her foolish fears, when the words froze on her lips.

This was not the Yahmose she knew—the gentle, kindly brother. His eyes were very bright and he was passing his tongue quickly over dried lips. His hands, held a little in front of his body, were slightly curved, the fingers looking like talons.

He was looking at her and the look in his eyes was unmistakable. It was the look of a man who had killed and was about to kill again. There was a gloating cruelty, an evil satisfaction in his face.

Yahmose—the pitiless enemy was Yahmose! Behind the mask of that gentle, kindly face—*this*!

She had thought that her brother loved her—but there was no love in that inhuman, gloating face.

Renisenb screamed—a faint, hopeless scream.

This, she knew, was death. There was no strength in her to match Yahmose's strength. Here, where Nofret had fallen, where the path was narrow, she too would fall to death . . .

'Yahmose!' It was a last appeal—in that uttering of his name was the love she had always given to this eldest brother. It pleaded in vain. Yahmose laughed, a soft, inhuman, happy little laugh.

Then he rushed forward, those cruel hands with

talons curving as though they longed to fasten round her throat . . .

Renisenb backed up against the cliff face, her hands outstretched in a vain attempt to ward him off. This was terror—death.

And then she heard a sound, a faint, twanging musical sound . . .

Something came singing through the air. Yahmose stopped, swayed, then with a loud cry he pitched forward on his face at her feet. She stared down stupidly at the feather shaft of an arrow. Then she looked down over the edge—to where Hori stood, the bow still held to his shoulder . . .

'Yahmose . . . Yahmose . . .'

Renisenb, numbed by the shock, repeated the name again, and yet again. It was as though she could not believe it . . .

She was outside the little rock chamber, Hori's arm still round her. She could hardly recollect how he had led her back up the path. She had been only able to repeat her brother's name in that dazed tone of wonder and horror.

Hori said gently:

'Yes, Yahmose. All the time, Yahmose.'

'But how? Why? And how *could* it be he—why, he was poisoned himself. He nearly died.'

'No, he ran no risk of dying. He was very careful of how much wine he drank. He sipped enough to make him ill and he exaggerated his symptoms and his pains. It was the way, he knew, to disarm suspicion.'

'But *he* could not have killed Ipy? Why, he was so weak he could not stand on his feet!'

'That, again, was feigned. Do you not remember that Mersu pronounced that once the poison was eliminated, he would regain strength quickly. So he did in reality.'

'But *why*, Hori? That is what I cannot make out—why?'

Hori sighed.

'Do you remember, Renisenb, that I talked to you once of the rottenness that comes from within?'

'I remember. Indeed I was thinking of it only this evening.'

'You said once that the coming of Nofret brought evil. That was not true. The evil was already here concealed within the hearts of the household. All that Nofret's coming did was to bring it from its hidden place into the light. Her presence banished concealment. Kait's gentle motherliness had turned to ruthless egoism for herself and her young. Sobek was no longer the gay and charming young man, but the boastful, dissipated weakling. Ipy was not so much a spoilt, attractive child as a scheming, selfish boy. Through Henet's pretended devotion, the venom began to show clearly. Satipy showed herself as a bully and a coward. Imhotep himself had degenerated into a fussy, pompous tyrant.'

'I know—I know.' Renisenb's hands went to rub her eyes. 'You need not tell me. I have found out little by little for myself . . . Why should these things happen—why should this rottenness come, as you say, working from within?'

Hori shrugged his shoulders.

'Who can tell? It may be that there must always be growth—and that if one does not grow kinder and wiser and greater, then the growth must be the other way, fostering the evil things. Or it may be that the life they all led was too shut in, too folded back upon itself—without breadth or vision. Or it may be that, like a disease of crops, it is contagious, that first one and then another sickened.'

'But Yahmose—Yahmose seemed always the same.'

'Yes, and that is one reason, Renisenb, why I came to suspect. For the others, by reason of their temperaments, could get relief. But Yahmose has always been timid, easily ruled, and with never enough courage to rebel. He loved Imhotep and worked hard to please him, and Imhotep found him well-meaning but stupid and slow. He despised him. Satipy, too, treated Yahmose with all of the scorn of a bullying nature. Slowly his burden of resentment, concealed but deeply felt, grew heavier. The meeker he seemed, the more his inward anger grew.

'And then, just when Yahmose was hoping at last to reap the reward of his industry and diligence, to be recognized and associated with his father, Nofret came. It was Nofret, and perhaps Nofret's beauty, that kindled the final spark. She attacked the manhood of all three brothers. She touched Sobek on the raw by her scorn of him as a fool, she infuriated Ipy by treating him as a truculent child without any claim to manhood, and she showed Yahmose that he was something less than a man in her eyes. It was after Nofret came that Satipy's tongue finally goaded Yahmose beyond endurance. It was her jeers, her taunt that she was a better man than he, that finally sapped his self-control. He met Nofret on this path and—driven beyond endurance—he threw her down.'

'But it was *Satipy*—'

'No, no, Renisenb. That is where you were all wrong. From down below Satipy *saw it happen*. Now do you understand?'

'But Yahmose was with you on the cultivation.'

'Yes, for the last hour. But do you not realize, Renisenb, that Nofret's body was *cold*? You felt her cheek yourself. You thought she had fallen a few moments before—but that was impossible. She had been dead at least two hours, otherwise, in that hot sun, her face could never have felt cold to your touch. Satipy saw it happen. Satipy hung around, fearful, uncertain what to do; then she saw you coming and tried to head you off.'

'Hori, when did you know all this?'

'I guessed fairly soon. It was Satipy's behaviour that told me. She was obviously going about in deadly fear of someone or something—and I was fairly soon convinced that the person she feared was *Yahmose*. She stopped bullying him and instead was eager to obey him in every way. It had been, you see, a terrible shock to her. Yahmose, whom she despised as the meekest of men, had actually been the one to kill Nofret. It turned Satipy's world upside down. Like most bullying women, she was a coward. This new Yahmose terrified her. In her fear she began to talk in her sleep. Yahmose soon realized that she was a danger to him . . .

'And now, Renisenb, you can realize the truth of what

you saw that day with your own eyes. It was not a spirit Satipy saw that caused her to fall. She saw what you saw today. She saw in the face of the man following her—her own husband—the intention to throw her down as he had thrown that other woman. In her fear she backed away from him and fell. And when, with her dying lips, she shaped the word *Nofret*, she was trying to tell you that Yahmose killed Nofret.'

Hori paused and then went on:

'Esa came on the truth because of an entirely irrelevant remark made by Henet. Henet complained that I did not look *at* her, but as though I saw something behind her that was not there. She went on to speak of Satipy. In a flash Esa saw how much simpler the whole thing was than we had thought. Satipy did not look at something *behind* Yahmose—it was *Yahmose himself* she saw. To test her idea, Esa introduced the subject in a rambling way which could mean nothing to anyone except Yahmose himself— and only to him if what she suspected was true. Her words surprised him and he reacted to them just for a moment, sufficiently for her to know that what she suspected was the truth. But Yahmose knew then that she *did* suspect. And once a suspicion had arisen, things would fit in too well, even to the story the herd boy told—a boy devoted to him who would do anything his Lord Yahmose commanded—even to swallowing a medicine that night which ensured that he would not wake up again . . .'

'Oh Hori, it is so hard to believe that Yahmose could do such things. Nofret, yes, I can understand that. But why these other killings?'

'It is difficult to explain to you, Renisenb, but once the heart is opened to evil—evil blossoms like poppies amongst the corn. All his life Yahmose had had, perhaps, a longing for violence and had been unable to achieve it. He despised his own meek, submissive role. I think that the killing of Nofret gave him a great sense of *power*. He realized it first by Satipy. Satipy who had browbeaten and abused him, was now meek and terrified. All the grievances that had lain buried in his heart so long, reared their heads—as that snake reared up on the path here one day. Sobek and Ipy were, one handsomer, the other cleverer than he—so *they* must go. He, Yahmose, was to be the ruler of the house, and his father's only comfort and stay! Satipy's death increased the actual pleasure of killing. He felt more powerful as a result of it. It was after that that his mind began to give way—from then on evil possessed him utterly.

'You, Renisenb, were not a rival. So far as he still could, he loved you. But the idea that your husband should share with him in the estate was not one to be borne. I think Esa agreed to the idea of accepting Kameni with two ideas in her head—the first that if Yahmose struck again, it would be more likely to be at Kameni than at you—and in any case she trusted me to see that you were kept safe. The second idea—for Esa was a bold woman—was to bring things to a head. Yahmose, watched by me (whom he did not know suspected him) could be caught in the act.'

'As you did,' said Renisenb. 'Oh Hori, I was so frightened when I looked back and saw him.'

'I know, Renisenb. But it had to be. So long as I stuck close to Yahmose's side, you would necessarily be safe—

but that could not go on for ever. I knew that if he had an opportunity of throwing you off the path *at the same place* he would take it. It would revive the superstitious explanation of the deaths.'

'Then the message Henet brought me was not from you?'

Hori shook his head.

'I sent you no message.'

'But why did Henet—' Renisenb stopped, and shook her head. 'I cannot understand Henet's part in all this.'

'I think Henet knows the truth,' said Hori thoughtfully. 'She was conveying as much to Yahmose this morning—a dangerous thing to do. He made use of her to lure you up here—a thing she would be willing to do—since she hates you, Renisenb—'

'I know.'

'Afterwards—I wonder? Henet would believe her knowledge would give her power. But I do not believe Yahmose would have let her live long. Perhaps even now—'

Renisenb shivered.

'Yahmose was mad,' said Renisenb. 'He was possessed by evil spirits, but he was not always like that.'

'No, and yet—You remember, Renisenb, how I told you the story of Sobek and Yahmose as children, and how Sobek beat Yahmose's head against the ground and how your mother came, all pale and trembling and said, "That is dangerous." I think, Renisenb, that her meaning was that to do such things *to Yahmose* was dangerous. Remember that next day how Sobek was ill—food poisoning, they thought—I think your mother, Renisenb, knew something of the queer self-contained fury that dwelt within the breast of her gentle, meek little son and feared that some day it might be roused . . .'

Renisenb shuddered.

'Is no one what they seem?'

Hori smiled at her.

'Yes, sometimes. Kameni and I, Renisenb. Both of us, I think, are as you believe we are. Kameni and I . . .'

He said the last words with significance, and suddenly Renisenb realized that she stood at a moment of choice in her life.

Hori went on:

'We both love you, Renisenb. You must know that.'

'And yet,' said Renisenb, slowly, 'you have let the arrangements be made for my marriage, and you have said nothing—not one word.'

'That was for your protection. Esa had the same idea. I must remain disinterested and aloof, so that I could keep constant watch on Yahmose, and not arouse his animosity.' Hori added with emotion: 'You must understand, Renisenb, that Yahmose has been my friend for many years. I loved Yahmose. I tried to induce your father to give him the status and authority he desired. I failed. All that came too late. But although I was convinced in my heart that Yahmose had killed Nofret, I tried *not* to believe it. I found excuses, even, for his action. Yahmose, my unhappy, tormented friend, was very dear to me. Then came Sobek's death, and Ipy, and finally Esa's . . . I knew then that the evil in Yahmose had finally vanquished the good. And so Yahmose has come to his death at my hands. A swift, almost painless death.'

'Death—always death.'

'No, Renisenb. It is not death that faces you today, but life. With whom will you share that life? With Kameni or with me?'

Renisenb stared straight ahead of her, out over the valley below and to the silver streak of the Nile.

Before her, very clearly, there rose up the image of Kameni's smiling face as he had sat facing her that day in the boat.

Handsome, strong, gay . . . She felt again the throb and lilt of her blood. She had loved Kameni in that moment. She loved him now. Kameni could take the place that Khay had held in her life.

She thought: 'We shall be happy together—yes, we shall be happy. We shall live together and take pleasure in each other and we shall have strong, handsome children. There will be busy days full of work . . . and days of pleasure when we sail on the river . . . Life will be again as I knew it with Khay . . . What could I ask more than that? What do I want more than that?'

And slowly, very slowly indeed, she turned her face towards Hori. It was as though, silently, she asked him a question.

As though he understood her, he answered:

'When you were a child, I loved you. I loved your grave face and the confidence with which you came to me, asking me to mend your broken toys. And then, after eight years' absence, you came again and sat here, and brought me the thoughts that were in your mind. And your mind, Renisenb is not like the minds of the rest of your family. It does no turn in upon itself, seeking to encase itself in narrow walls. Your mind is like my mind, it looks over the river, seeing a world of changes, of new ideas—seeing a world where all things are possible to those with courage and vision . . .'

'I know, Hori, I know. I have felt these things with you. But not all the time. There will be moments when I cannot follow you, when I shall be alone . . .'

She broke off, unable to find words to frame her struggling thoughts. What life would be with Hori, she did not know. In spite of his gentleness, in spite of his love for her, he would remain in some respects incalculable and incomprehensible. They would share moments of great beauty and richness together—but what of their common daily life?

She stretched out her hands impulsively to him.

'Oh, Hori, decide for me. Tell me what to do!'

He smiled at her, at the child Renisenb speaking, perhaps, for the last time. But he did not take her hands.

'*I* cannot tell you what to do with your life, Renisenb— because it is *your* life—and only you can decide.'

She realized then that she was to have no help, no quickening appeal to her senses such as Kameni had made. If Hori would only have touched her—but he did not touch her.

And the choice suddenly presented itself to her in the simplest terms—the easy life or the difficult one. She was strongly tempted then to turn and go down the winding path, down to the normal, happy life she already knew— that she had experienced before with Khay. There was safety there—the sharing of daily pleasures and griefs with nothing to fear but old age and death . . .

Death . . . From thoughts of life she had come full circle again to death. Khay had died. Kameni, perhaps, would die, and his face, like Khay's, would slowly fade from her memory . . .

She looked then at Hori standing quietly beside her. It was odd, she thought, that she had never really known just what Hori looked like . . . She had never needed to know . . .

She spoke then, and the tone of her voice was the same as when she had announced, long before, that she would walk down the path at sunset alone.

'I have made my choice, Hori. I will share my life with you for good or evil, until death comes . . .'

With his arms round her, with the sudden new sweetness of his face against hers, she was filled with an exultant richness of living.

'If Hori were to die,' she thought, 'I should *not* forget! Hori is a song in my heart for ever . . . That means—that there is no more death . . .'

THE END